Whispers

by

Zack Rose

DORRANCE
PUBLISHING CO
EST. 1920
PITTSBURGH, PENNSYLVANIA 15238

Dorrance Publishing Co
585 Alpha Drive
Pittsburgh, PA 15238
Visit our website at *www.dorrancebookstore.com*

ISBN: 978-1-6453-0692-4
eISBN: 978-1-6453-0320-6

This book is dedicated to:

Alice B. Lewis for 44 years of support in writing this book.

Zack Rose

Whispers

Table of Contents

Chapter 1

Jake Rose made his way up the beaten path, a path he had traveled many times. He shifted the load he carried, a burlap bag filled with apples. He had always loved apples and with the winter coming on he had spent the previous weeks gathering what the earth had so graciously blessed him with. Jake loved the mountain and everything that dwelled within it. His problem was with the two-legged creatures that seemed to mire the beauty of his surroundings. He had long since determined that they would be the downfall to their existence.

As he made his way up the trail, he paused at a fallen chestnut tree. It had found its final resting place there many years ago. The majestic trees had been glamorous in their time until a disease had blown through and wiped them out. In the early part of the 19th century, the timber from the great trees had been used for many things, from building homes and barns to split rails for fences. Most all the structure had been torn down for the lumber and the price for "wormy chestnut," named for all the holes in the lumber cut by worms, had been sold for as much as six dollars a board foot. A lot of rich people had bought the lumber to put in their homes or summer homes they might have here in the mountains, another thing that Jake frowned upon.

Jake set his bag of apples down and lowered his 6'5" frame onto a natural seat between two sections of the chestnut tree and a stump from a chestnut oak that had been long cut for firewood. Wilson, a three-year-old black pug that Jake had rescued from the dog pound, eased up to his feet and plopped down breathing hard, tongue hanging out like a leaf under the weight of a spring rain. Jake took in the beauty of his surroundings and felt a slight breeze blowing. It was the middle of October and the leaves were starting to change. He loved this time of year. It was what followed him that bothered him. Jake pulled the can of Prince Albert from his pocket and rolled a smoke as he looked out over the valley where he grew up

As a child of the '50s, the winters had been rough and they had seemed to go on forever. His thoughts went back to those days, the old house they had lived in where sometimes it felt colder in the house than outside. He thought of his mom trying to keep the house warm and her burned hands from feeding a never satisfied coal heater. Jake's dad had died when he was young and their lives after that had been, to Jake, in some ways what he thought hell might be like. He had to force his mind back to the present, when his memories took him where everything seemed to all run together. He would go there later, but not now.

Wilson had fallen asleep at his feet and was snoring softly. Jake thought of resuming his chores that had to be done, but sat for a few minutes more. Age and gravity were becoming his worst adversary. He had just turned 56 and he felt it. The countless ear infections as a child had robbed him of the best part of his hearing and his back had long since said "no more."

Jake sat for a time savoring the mid-October weather, and the day was warm enough that he only had on a light flannel shirt. He made the walk to the few remaining apple trees that his grandfather had planted years before. Most everything was gone now, and only remnants of the old house were still visible. Most of the land had fallen victim to the wild rose bushes and pine trees. Jake had always wanted to fix the place back up and build a new barn, but time had slipped away from him. As a child, he had wandered the mountain, found a knoll overlooking the valley below, and vowed that someday he would build a cabin overlooking the place where he had grown up. Through the years, with a little help from a friend, he had constructed a cabin just big enough for one person.

Jake loved the old ways and to look at the cabin it would appear to have been built in the early part of the 19th century. The road that led to the cabin left a lot to be desired and Jake liked it that way. His old Willys Jeep seemed to make the trip just fine. From his pocket he drew a small medicine bottle and downed two painkillers with the water he had gotten at the old spring where, as a child, he had carried many a pail of water. His back was bothering him from the walk up from the orchard.

Jake shifted his weight and started to get up when he noticed the breeze picking up. He studied a small maple tree just below the trail and the leaves seemed to move in no certain direction as if they were confused as to which direction the wind was blowing. Jake stood and looked farther down the mountain to a giant oak tree and there seemed to be no wind moving any of the branches. The wind had a strange sound to it. It seemed to be everywhere but yet nowhere. Jake looked down and saw that Wilson was now standing with the hair on his back standing straight up. Jake looked around and noticed that the wind was confined to the area surrounding where he stood. The flannel shirt Jake was wearing had become inadequate for the chill he was feeling. It seemed that the temperature had dropped at least 10 degrees. Wilson moved in front of Jake and seemed unsure of what he should do.

"Wilson, what is it?" His own voice sounded different, as if it held an echo.

The dog never responded and only kept staring up the trail. From somewhere Jake detected a shallow moan that seemed to come from all directions. He had never been one to scare easily, but he felt a tingle run up his spine and he shuddered. He stood riveted to the spot where he stood and was unable to take his eyes away from the trail that led to his home. As quickly as it had happened, the air was still and Jake realized the breeze had died down. He stood for a few minutes more before turning to look back down the trail. The maple tree was still and he noticed the chill in the air had subsided. Wilson had retreated back against Jake's feet as if nothing had happened.

Jake studied the surrounding forest and the only thing he noticed was a squirrel scampering up the fallen chestnut tree with an acorn. The experience had unnerved him and, being Jake, he desperately looked for some explanation. Being a former police officer he had encountered many things, but nothing like this. For a few moments, he wished that he had taken the pistol he kept in the dresser drawer, and then dismissed the idea. He had no clue as to what had just happened and if a weapon would have done any good to an unseen force. He thought of the moan he had heard and tried desperately to put a meaning to it. Was somebody there? Were they hurt? Jake had chosen this place to be as far away from people as he could get, and now it seemed as if something was invading his privacy. He thought about yelling out but changed his mind. He wanted to investigate first, before making his presence known.

He moved up the trail leaving his bag of apples behind. The only weapon he carried was a hunting knife that he drew and kept close to his side. As he made his way up the trail, Wilson stayed right at his heels. It was still a ways to the cabin and he moved slowly along the trail, every so often looking and checking from side to side. He thought of how strange the moan had sounded, and his inability to tell what direction it came from puzzled him. His hearing hadn't helped and he seemed to be at a loss.

Jake's family had moved to this place many years ago. In the late 1800s, his grandfather Turner Rose had come down from the mountains of West Virginia and settled in the Rocky Creek area of Judson, North Carolina. Jake knew little about him other than the stories his father Jasper had told him as a child. He had listened to his father tell the story about the trip down and how many months it took them to travel by horse and wagon and how Jake's great aunt, Laura Mills, had died on the trip and was buried somewhere along the road.

Jake's father, Jasper Rose, at the ripe old age of 55, married Anella Blake after his wife passed away. There had been two daughters from the previous marriage, and when Jasper married Anella Blake they were old enough to be Jake's mom. Anella Blake was 20 years Jasper's senior and was a beautiful woman who was part Cherokee. Jake had learned a lot about her culture as he had grown up. In the few good memories Jake had of her as a child, he remembered her talking about her people and how rough her childhood had been. It wasn't until her death in 1988 that Jake learned how bad her life had been before marrying Jasper Rose.

At the funeral, Jake's aunt, Rena Morgan, had tried to explain to him the things that had happened to her as a child: how her own father had raped her when she was 10; that later on, as an adult, she had been raped again, and that somewhere out there he had a half-sister. The child had been named Anella after her mother. When she couldn't take care of her, she had been given up for adoption at the age of four. She had tried to raise Jake as best as she could, but the demons from her past hindered her ability to do so.

After Jasper had passed away from years of smoking, Jake's life had gone from bad to worse. There had been nights when he had woken up to find a house full of men drinking and his mom passed out from all the booze. He would hide in the closet in the back room and stay throughout the night, crying until he went back to sleep. He remembered on one occasion coming in the old house and finding the bed on fire from a cigarette his mom had lit before passing out.

Jake's half-brother and sister had tried to help by taking Jake in the summer and trying to help with raising him. But it would only be for a short time because they had trouble handling him, so they would bring him back. To say the least, Jake Rose was a very troubled child.

As Jake made his way up the trail cautiously, he stopped often to survey his surroundings. Everything seemed the same, but he was having a hard time shaking the feeling that something wasn't right. He had never been superstitious and the stories he had heard as a child had never had much effect on him. He always figured the stories he heard were told to scare kids into staying out of trouble. Even though he couldn't hide that, he was scared when he walked in the dark down the road from the Binion family's home where he would go to play with JJ and Benny Binion.

Jake had heard the story of the man who was killed on the road and was beaten so badly that they had found his head a ways from the body. The story goes that Theo Carpenter had laid in wait for Thad Bryson, shot him first and then took a rock and beat him until his head had been severed from his body. It was told that Thad Bryson walked the road at night looking for his head.

As Jake neared the clearing where his cabin sat, he paused. Everything looked okay. The chickens seemed content pecking around the yard. Jake moved into the yard and turned to look back down the trail. Wilson had stopped at the edge of the yard and was staring towards Jake. That seemed unusual because Wilson would usually beat him to the front porch where Dexter, an 11-year-old Bluetick hound, was usually asleep. Jake had had Dexter since he was a puppy, but now, in his old age, Dexter usually didn't go with Jake in the woods.

Jake surveyed everything. It all seemed to be in place. His old Willys Jeep sat behind the cabin undisturbed. He looked past the cabin to the hog lot and saw that both pigs were sleeping soundly. Jake made his way to the porch, and Dexter raised his head and gave a few wags of his tail.

"Some watch dog you are," Jake said out loud and patted him on the head.

Jake looked back, and Wilson had ventured out a few feet into the yard. He is really acting strange, Jake thought. He had heard the stories, and believed most of them, about how animals could sense things that people couldn't. But why wasn't Dexter acting any different?

Jake usually left both doors on the cabin unlocked, and today hadn't been any different. He slowly opened the screen door and eased inside keeping his back to the open door. He had left the radio on and an old song Jake loved "You've Never Been This Far Before" by Conway Twitty was playing.

Over the years that Jake had spent building the cabin, he had tried to make it look as old as he could. He had torn down old houses and barns. He had pulled the logs out with "Brutus," as he called the machine he had built over 20 years ago. Brutus had once been a school bus that the new preacher from the church just below where Jake had lived for the past 25 years had gotten donated to the church. An attempted trip to Abbeyville had failed when he tried to pick a drink up from the floor of the bus and drove the bus into a rock wall. Hardy Jackson was okay, but the bus was totaled and somewhere along the way was given to Jake, who turned it into something that looked like a leftover from the movie *Road Warrior*.

Jake thought of his medicine that he kept hidden in case someone came in unexpectedly and started asking questions that he did not want to have to explain. He pulled the small wooden box from its hiding place and made a survey of its contents. He checked his pain meds first, knowing that would be the first thing someone would take if his hiding place had been discovered. Everything was there and he breathed a sigh of relief. His antidepressants were there – the drugs he had been on for most of his adult life – along with his sleeping pills and blood pressure meds. He returned the box to its hiding place. His thoughts returned to his mom and all the medicine she had taken, the antipsychotic drugs Tofarnil and Mellaril; the scar on her arm that she had told Jake was from a car accident, but that Jake learned after her death was from a suicide attempt. Jake had struggled with suicidal feelings most of his life. His earliest memory was when he was 16 years old sitting in the old house trying to slit his wrist with a razor blade.

Jake surveyed everything in the cabin, mentally checking them off his list. Everything seemed to be in order. Through the back door he could see Brutus sitting waiting for whatever endeavor Jake might choose to do later. He glanced back out the front door and noticed that Wilson had made his way to the front porch and was stretched out beside Dexter. Jake made his way to the back porch and chased the chickens away that had gathered in anticipation of him feeding them some of the cracked corn he kept in the small shed adjacent to the cabin. He stopped next to the Willys Jeep and reminded himself that he had to make a trip to Judson to replace the two front tires on the Jeep that provided transport up and down the steep road from his home to Rocky Creek Road. Jake always hated going into town and seemed to always wait until he was out of everything before making the trip.

Jake moved from the back porch toward the barn and stopped at the hog pen. His thoughts were still on what had happened earlier and wondering where the voice had come from. He couldn't really say it was a female voice, but it sure sounded female, almost that of a small girl.

He thought of his bag of apples that he left behind and almost dreaded the thought of venturing back down the trail to retrieve them. He glanced down at "Jed and Clampett," the two hogs his granddaughter Sarah had named.

"Well, boys, it's close to the time to send you to the Promised Land," Jake said aloud.

Jake casually checked his watch. He could have sworn that the old grandfather clock in the cabin showed 4:15 p.m. However, his watch only showed 3:48 p.m., so either his watch was wrong or he had lost approximately 30 minutes. Jake checked the watch that had been passed down to him from his father. He attempted to wind the old watch, but after three turns the stem was snug. He checked his cell phone, which showed the time to be 30 minutes faster than the watch. He dismissed the difference in time considering the age of the watch and made a mental note to get the watch checked the next time he was in town.

As Jake moved toward the barn, he thought of his five wonderful grandchildren who his son James, named after his great uncle who fought in the Civil War, had blessed him with. Jasper Rose, named after Jake's dad, was now 11 years old, and it seemed like yesterday that they were all at the hospital when he was born. Kala and Sarah were three years apart, Kala eight and Sarah five. The two girls were a handful and many times had tried Jake's patience. The grandkids could never understand why Papaw had to live back in the woods and not at home with Mamaw.

In 1996, Jake and Alona had adopted a child and named him after Alona's dad, Victor Bearmeat. Alona and Jake had known Victor's parents for years, and after Janie Matheson, Victor's mom, had passed away from a long bout with cancer, Victor's dad, Manny Matheson, came to Jake and Alona and said he felt his son would be better off with them. Victor, who was so much like Jake it was scary, clung to him like Jake was his real father. Victor spent a lot of time with Jake on the mountain, and Jake taught him a lot of the things that he had learned as a child. If it was up to Victor, he would live on the mountain with Jake forever.

Jake was far from the perfect husband and had let Alona down more times than he could count. He would have bouts of depression that would sometimes seem to last for years. His ability to hold down a job had always been an issue, and the job as a police officer with the Town of Judson had been the longest time he had held one. Alona and Jake finally parted ways in 2005 and Jake moved to his cabin to live. Alona never liked where Jake had built the cabin and could not understand why someone would want to live so close to where their life had been hell as a child.

Jake had always been somewhat of a jack of all trades and had built a water wheel over the stream that ran on the back side of the ridge that his cabin sat on. He had designed a generator to provide electricity for the cabin and the barn. Jake smiled at the idea of not having to use the power from Allen Power Company, anything to keep from feeding their greedy hand. Jake had come to the conclusion that the greed in the world had become so great that it had surpassed any point of understanding the oil companies that literally had the world by its balls, jobs that had been lost to companies overseas, and with little regard to the American people. That was another reason that Jake went as far away from people as he could get.

Jake had designed his cabin to be almost self-sufficient, heating and cooking with wood. His garden had done great this year and he had canned and preserved what he would need to see him through the winter. With cold weather almost upon him, he would slaughter Jed and Clampett and take the meat to town to be ground up for sausage and have pork chops cut at the slaughter house. He would try and explain to Sarah and Kala that Jed and Clampett had gone to heaven and someday they would see them again.

Jake moved on toward the barn and threw a block of hay to Commander, his four-year-old gelding Saddlebred horse. The horse nudged Jake's hand and pulled at his shirt pocket where sometimes he would put an apple.

"Sorry, Bud," Jake said softly, "no apple today."

Jake stood in the small barn that he had constructed some years ago and took in the aroma of the hay and thought about the time his father had cut hay with a horse-drawn mowing machine. Jake had managed to keep the old mower and had put it on the hill next to the barn, more to look at than use it like his daddy had.

As Jake stood in the doorway of the barn, something moved off to his left. Jake froze still, unnerved by what had happened. He desperately searched the area below the cabin for what had caught his attention. Nothing moved and the only sound was the horse munching the hay. Jake sometimes wondered if all the medicine that he had taken over the years would come back to haunt him later and was now questioning the possibility that he had imagined everything that had happened earlier.

Wilson joined Jake at the barn, and Jake noticed that the dog was intently looking at the place where Jake thought something had moved. Wilson's hair was standing up on his back like before, and when Jake spoke to him he acted like he didn't even hear him. Just the sight of Wilson with his hair on end concerned Jake, so he searched the area below more intently. Wilson took two steps back and was now against Jake's leg. Jake felt the dog trembling and reached down to pet him, but when he touched him, the dog gave a yelp and ran back in the barn. With Jake's concern growing more rapidly, he also backed up.

"Good Lord," Jake said out loud, "what is happening?"

Still nothing moved, and after what seemed like hours Wilson moved back to the entrance of the barn and stood looking back down the hill. Jake called out, and Wilson turned and wagged his tail and moved over to where Jake stood.

Chapter 2

Jake had married Alona Bearmeat, a full blood Cherokee, in 1974, and four years later James had been born. As the years went by, they had come to the conclusion that James was going to be the only child that God was going to bless them with.

Jake thought back to the night that he had totaled his cruiser on Sycamore Road. He had been working the night shift and received a call of an intoxicated driver and the description of the car. Jake located it just outside Judson. He followed the car for some time and attempted to stop it on Sycamore Road. The car, an old Chevy Chevelle, sped away when Jake turned on his blue lights. He chased Jerry Jeffries, a teenager, for some distance, when he lost control of his cruiser after hitting an ice patch and flipped the car in Sycamore Creek.

Jake spent three months in Judson Hospital with a broken pelvis and crushed vertebrae. Dr. Jarrett had informed him that his days as a police officer were over. Jake had gone through days of pain, and after a slow recovery applied for Social Security disability. After a grueling two years and many trips to the lawyer, he received his back pay and would receive a monthly check. It wasn't much, but he felt better knowing that he would be helping the family on a monthly basis.

Jake slipped the can of Prince Albert from his pocket and with ease rolled a smoke. He stood a while longer savoring the effect of his first smoke since picking the apples earlier. As he thought of his dad who died from years of smoking cigarettes, he tried to make a mental note to cut back on his own smoking. He had battled the addiction of nicotine for years and had successfully quit for two years, but fell victim to the habit after gaining so much weight that he had to replace his entire wardrobe and found it a difficult task to bend over to tie his shoe. His blood pressure had gone outrageously high, and Dr. Jarrett had warned him that he was close to having a stroke. So Jake had chosen, as he put it, the lesser of two evils.

After much thought Jake made his way back down the trail and retrieved the sack of apples. On the trip back up, he questioned what had happened earlier and tried to remember exactly how the childlike moan had sounded. He searched his memory for something that sounded the same. It wasn't until Jake had deposited the apples on the front porch that he remembered where he had heard that sound. Years earlier, he and Alona had been at a funeral of Alona's family and he had heard a small child weeping over the death of her grandmother. The cry the small child made sounded so much like the sound Jake had witnessed earlier. He had never entertained the idea of places being haunted and always believed there was an explanation to everything. Jake thought back to when he had first built his cabin and let some friends of theirs spend the night in it. Linda and George Atkins had come back with a story of hearing things and had taken a picture inside the cabin. Linda had shown Jake the picture she had taken of George and what she said looked like something just behind him on the stairs that led up to the bedroom. Jake had dismissed this as something in the film or on the camera lens. Jake had spent many nights there and never experienced anything out of the ordinary.

Jake spent the evening fixing the apples and removing the outer covering from some black walnuts he had gathered earlier. Wilson was beginning to emit a dirty dog smell, so Jake heated a pail of water and proceeded to give "Turd" a bath. Wilson had earned the nickname "Turd" for the many times he had crapped in the house while Jake was trying to housebreak him. Wilson retreated to the far corner of the living room after seeing Jake getting out of the small washtub that he used to bathe him in. After some time and water all over the kitchen floor, Wilson was once more worthy to sleep at the foot of Jake's bed. Jake retreated to his recliner, his back hurting, and washed down two more painkillers. As he closed his eyes and was thinking again of the events that had consumed a big part of his day, a pungent odor invaded his sense of smell.

"Goodness, Wilson, what have you been eating?"

Wilson, knowing what he had done, cautiously moved to the far corner of the room and plopped down as if in pain. Jake eyed Wilson and thought how much company the little fellow had been to him. He had chosen Wilson for the white spot on his chest and had grown very fond of him very quickly. Jake was still puzzled over the fact that Wilson had detected something before Dexter, the Bluetick hound who was a born hunter.

Jake arose and made his way to the kitchen to prepare supper, as he called it. Most of the foreigners that had gradually seemed to invade every part of Abbey County called it "breakfast, lunch and dinner." Jake had always believed lunch and dinner were the same and supper came at the end of the day. Well, he was old-fashioned and didn't give a rat's ass what anyone thought about him, especially someone who had come to this area with all their money and building fancy houses on the highest mountain they could find. Jake smiled as he thought of what his mom had said when he was a child: "Those people are trying to get as close to heaven as they can."

Jake's thoughts were interrupted by the jingle of his cell phone. He checked the caller ID and saw that it was Alona's phone.

"Hello?"

"Hey, Papaw" – Jake recognized the voice of his grandson Jasper – "me and Victor want to come spend the weekend with you. Please, Papaw," he pleaded.

Jake thought for a moment before speaking.

"Well, we will have to wait and see. Are you boys doing good in school?"

"Oh, yeah, Papaw," Jasper exclaimed. "I got three A's on my report card and Victor got two."

"Well," Jake said, "we will see what we can do. Okay?"

"Okay, Papaw," Jasper said in a hopeful voice. "Hold on. Victor wants to talk to you."

Victor, now 14, spoke in a more adult tone. "Is it about time to kill the hogs, Dad?"

"Well, Victor," Jake responded, "it's really close."

"Can I shoot them?" Victor asked.

"Well, we will have to see about that," Jake said.

Jake had taken Victor hunting with him and he shot his first squirrel at the age of 13. Jake bought Victor a single-shot rifle, and Victor seemed to be quick to learn how dangerous guns can be if not used properly.

"Hey, Dad," Victor said, "Mom wants to talk to you."

Jake cringed, not really wanting to speak to her at that very second. Her voice could sometimes bring Jake down, and he didn't need that right now.

"Hello, Jake," Alona spoke in a not so warm voice. "How you doing up there in that God forsaken place?"

"Just dandy," Jake answered back in a tone to counteract hers. "I been busy getting ready for the cold weather."

Damn, he thought, *she gets under my skin at times.*

His dependency on her over the years had only added to the way Jake felt about himself. The abuse Jake had suffered as a child had left him with no confidence in himself, and he had fought with the depression and the suicide attempt so long that all had robbed him of a way to cope with life in general and the duties that were required of him as a husband and an adult. He had been through extensive counseling through his adult years and had finally been able to talk about his childhood. He hadn't been to counseling in a long time and deep down he knew he should. It seemed like every time he would get a good counselor and it seemed to be working, they would leave or try to send him to someone else. The best counselor he could remember having was Tom Hollbrook, who had helped him the most. But at one session, Tom told him he was moving to Myrtle Beach, South Carolina, to be with his girlfriend. Jake had been devastated and vowed never to see anyone as long as he lived.

"Well, Jake," Alona said, "these kids don't understand why you are not here. And we did agree to go to marriage counseling a long time ago and we haven't gone once."

"Yes, I know," Jake replied, "and we will soon."

Jake changed the subject to ask how everyone was doing and how his son was doing in college where he was taking computer programming, something Jake was completely lost about and had trouble even working his cell phone.

"Don't change the subject, Jake," Alona interrupted him in a tone that could melt ice.

"Okay, okay," he replied, trying to sound like he was listening to her. "We will go to counseling and I will try to talk to the kids."

James, who had always taken his mom's side when an argument erupted, told Jake that what he decided to do was love him no matter the outcome.

"Okay, Alona", Jake said, "you set up an appointment with the marriage people and I will be there."

Jake spoke more with Alona about goings-on across the county and finally hung up promising one more time to go to marriage counseling.

Alona had been good to him, and when he had decided to move to the cabin she had told him she would wait while he figured out what he was going to do. And she had asked him, before they hung up, if he was taking his medicine and if he was happy up there on the mountain, a question Jake didn't really have an answer for.

Jake had wanted to tell Alona what had happened earlier, but refrained from doing so due to the way she had been raised with stories of Shillies that Jake believed were told to children to scare them into being good. Shillies and boogers and the little people were stories that Jake had heard his entire married life with Alona. Alona had explained that they believed the little people lived in the woods and under the house and came out at night and were mischievous and played tricks on you. Some of them were good and some were really mean and would sneak up on girls and pull their hair or pinch them. Jake figured, after he told Alona what had happened, she would tell him that it could be the spirits of old that roamed the mountains, and he was in no mood to listen to all that.

Jake sat staring out the window overlooking the valley below, sipping on a cup of black coffee. His rest had been fitful even after downing a handful of sleeping pills and antidepressants. He woke numerous times during the night, but the only sound he could hear was Wilson's snoring. The sun was just starting up when Jake moved to the front porch. The air had a chill to it, so Jake built a fire and fixed a small breakfast consisting of country ham and eggs.

He stood in the early morning light and thought about what had happened the night before. He couldn't help but notice the stillness that hung over the mountain. Then he realized the chickens were not moving around and he hadn't heard any of the roosters crowing. Dexter was still in his house, which was not like him at all. It seemed like the entire mountain was paralyzed and he was the only thing moving.

Jake moved down the steps and slowly moved across the yard. He turned and looked back at the cabin, his gaze rising to the chimney.

The smoke rising from the chimney seemed to hang in the air and Jake felt a chill run up his spine.

"What the hell is happening?" Jake said out loud, his voice sounding dead like it wasn't even his own.

Something brushed Jake's leg and he jumped, only to find out it was Dexter, who had moved out of his house and was standing next to Jake.

"Goodness!" Jake said, "Dexter, you scared the crap out of me." Dexter wagged his tail as if to say "I'm sorry."

Jake made his way to the chicken house and opened the gate to the fence that ran the length of the pen and made his way to gather what eggs had been laid the day before. There were usually seven or eight eggs, but after checking he couldn't find a one in any of the nests.

That's strange, he thought. *Maybe a possum got in or some other varmint cleaned them out.*

The chickens seemed to be on edge like they get when a chicken hawk is nearby. Jake stood for a while trying to put everything together, the wind on the trail, the voice he had heard that sounded like a child, Wilson's behavior, and now it seemed like his chickens had quit laying. He walked back and threw some corn on the ground, but the chickens made no move to follow him. Jake stood for a while trying to make some sense of what was happening and was lost in thought to the day before.

After some time he returned to the cabin. And by then Wilson wanted out and ran to promptly pee on the Jeep tire. After deliberating for a while, Jake decided to make the trip to town because he was low on coffee and other essential things he had to have.

After feeding Commander and turning him out in the pasture, he locked up the cabin and loaded Wilson in the Jeep and headed down the mountain. Jake had restored the old Willys in the shop that he had built adjacent to the barn. The old Willys chugged along, her engine purring like a kitten. The talents that Jake had acquired over the years enabled him to do a lot of things that other people couldn't. He often wondered what his life would have been like without doing his work at one thing for any length of time.

In the early 1980s, Jake had driven a truck over the road and had seen a lot of places, until the depression had won over and he couldn't do it anymore. He hated that part of himself and had thought seriously about committing suicide by driving the semi into a rock wall.

Shaking his head to clear his thoughts, Jake noticed that things seemed to be returning to normal. The chickens had finally come out before Jake left and hurriedly cleaned up the corn that he had put out for them. Then Jake realized something. The cats ... where were they? He thought back to yesterday and couldn't remember seeing either one of them. Curly and Moe, as Kala had named them, had shown up one day and never left. Jake thought of going back and trying to locate them, but made a mental note to look for them when he got back.

As Jake made his way down the mountain, he stopped at a point on the road where he could see the entire valley below. He could see the old Binion place where, as a child, he had spent many a day. He thought of Elmer and Hazel Binion and how many times they had fed him as a child when Jake's mom had been too drunk to cook for him and he would go up there and eat. The food had never been fancy, mostly potatoes and beans, and sometimes, when Elmer had killed a hog, they would have fresh meat. Elmer and Hazel had both passed away years ago, and Benny had been killed in a car wreck and JJ had passed away some years ago from a brain tumor.

Jake thought a moment and almost said out loud, "everybody that I knew as a child is gone and all the old people that were old when I was young are gone, too." He felt a deep sense of being alone and had to choke back the tears.

From where he stood, he could see most of the 480 acres that had been passed down to him from his grandfather. His older half-brother and half-sister had their homes in Tennessee and had never seemed interested in being in Judson. Jake very seldom spoke with them and had always felt that he had been labeled as the black sheep of the family. When Jake had spent time with them as a child, they always seemed to want to fix him in the short time he would spend with them. Jake figured they thought he was a bad influence on their two kids, Cindy and Becky.

Well, anyway, Jake thought, *they don't have to worry about that anymore.*

The two girls were both alcoholics and had been to rehab more times than Wilson had fleas on his butt.

Jake stood for a few minutes more looking farther down the valley. He could see the fancy homes of the rich people who had invaded the county and felt a sense of relief that his land bordered the Forest Service and, at least in his lifetime, none of them were getting a foot on his property.

As Jake continued on down the mountain road, he thought of his mom and how he would get so angry at her when he would come home and find her drunk or already passed out. After she died, he would sometimes go to her grave and sit for hours talking to her. There were so many unanswered questions that he had and he wasn't any closer to the answers now than 20 years ago. Jake's aunt, Rena Morgan, had tried to give Jake as much information about her as she could, and now she was gone too.

When Jake neared the old home place, he stopped and got a drink of water from the spring that he used to carry water from. He always thought it was the best water he had ever tasted. He hated the taste of the bottled water that all the stores sold. As he was getting back in the Jeep, he noticed a car had pulled up in the road. Jake recognized Glenn James, a police officer with the tribal police.

"Hello, Jake," Glen said as he walked up to where Jake was parked. "You finally decide to come off the hill?"

"Yeah, I reckon," Jake replied. "Got to go pick up some supplies from town. How's business?"

"Oh, you know, same old same old," Glenn replied. "Same drunks and same bullshit for the past 10 years."

Glenn James had helped Jake some on his days off when he was building his cabin and barn. They had been friends for years, and Jake had assisted him on some cases when he worked on the Judson PD.

"You miss the police work, Jake?" Glenn asked.

"Well, sometimes, for about 30 seconds, then I get over it," Jake replied as both of them burst out laughing.

"I want to ask you something, Glenn. Do you believe in ghosts?"

"Well," Glenn replied, "I know there are things out there that we can't explain and I've seen a few odd things in my time. Why do you ask?"

"Well, Glenn, things have been kind of strange up on the hill and I can't explain any of it."

"Well, Jake, don't you remember when I was helping you build the cabin and told you something just didn't feel right, as if something was trying to stop us from working up there?"

Jake thought back to one day and how a log, after being secured, had somehow rolled off and almost hit Glenn.

"You know, Jake, it's been said that there were burial grounds somewhere on the mountain and bad things have happened to people who disturbed them."

"Well, Glenn," Jake replied, "it would be my luck to have built the cabin right on top of one of them."

Jake and Glenn talked for a short while until Glenn got a call to go to the Judson Sheriff's Department. One good thing, Jake thought, was that the tribal police and the county seemed to work good together.

Jake set out for Judson after letting Wilson out to again pee on the tire. It was 16 miles to Judson and Jake took his time checking out what might have changed since his last trip to town. He passed a new home going up and wondered why someone would want a house so big you could get lost in it.

Jake figured he would get the tires put on the Jeep first. When he pulled up to Willy's Tire, the only place in Judson to get tires, he found Buckeye Bush just finishing up on one of the county vehicles. Buckeye looked up and greeted Jake.

"Well, hello, mountain man. You finally decide to come off the hill for a spell?"

Buckeye Bush had been a friend of Jake's for years, and he reminded Jake of Grizzly Adams, with his beard and the massive shoulders he had acquired from years of throwing tires around. Jake appreciated the idea that Buckeye was a friend, because he was someone that Jake wouldn't want as an enemy or to have to meet in a dark alley.

After some conversing about local happenings, two new tires on the Jeep and promising to come back to get the other two replaced, Jake headed out to the only grocery store in Judson. BiLow's had moved into Judson in the late '80s and had literally put all the small grocery stores out of business. Jake hated this, but there was nothing he could do about it and chalked it up to progress for the small town of Judson. Hard to compete with the big food companies, Jake thought.

He remembered going with his dad to Hooper's Store and how he would watch the butcher as he prepared the meat after they had killed a hog or a beef cow. Jake missed those times and how getting a piece of candy was the best part of his day.

Jake pulled into BiLow's parking lot. After checking his list and realizing that he had failed to feed the hogs before he had left earlier, it made him realize how all the things that had been happening on the mountain were really getting to him. He sat in the Jeep surveying the parking lot and thought of how he hated going in BiLow's. The parking lot was full, which made him uneasy because sometimes he would have trouble being around a lot of people, knowing how the ones that knew him would be asking questions that he didn't feel like answering. It was another reason he liked being by himself.

The store was full and Jake made his way to each side, checking his list and trying to fill his buggy as fast as he could. He was putting flour in the buggy and noticed a lady with her back to him. She seemed vaguely familiar and, when she turned, he recognized her. It was Judy Grasson, one of his old counselors. Jake had seen her for over three years and she had helped him through a lot of painful memories.

Judy recognized Jake and, after giving him a hug and asking how things were, informed him that she had moved back to Judson and was going to start to see patients again. Jake filled her in on his move to Rocky Creek to the old homestead and how he had finally built the cabin that he had talked so much about. They talked for a few minutes more, and after promising to get an appointment with her he resumed his shopping.

The checkout line was full and after what seemed like hours he was headed back to the Jeep. He climbed in feeling thankful that that chore was over. He had gotten lucky in BiLow's, only running into two people he knew and keeping the conversation with them short.

He thought about Judy Grasson and how he really needed to see her, all the things that had happened in the last two days that he needed to talk about. He had even explored the possibility that he had imagined all of it. That thought scared him more than he wanted to admit. There were so many things that he couldn't remember about his childhood, and sometimes he wasn't really sure that he wanted to.

Jake knew that sometimes the mind will block a traumatized experience and to unlock that is almost impossible. He thought of all the antidepressants he had taken over the years trying to find one that would work for him, and how he had ended up in the hospital after taking the antidepressant Effexor. That one had been a nightmare, with the uncontrollable tremors and panic attacks. After that, Jake had been careful about what he was taking and finally found some relief in the drug Lexapro, which he had been on now for a year and a half.

After two pain pills, Jake headed to the feed store and then to Dent's Cafe for a quick lunch before his last stop at Mark's Convenience Store for gas.

The cafe was empty except for an elderly couple in the corner booth, and Jake slid into a table next to the window. Willow Reid emerged from the back and gave Jake a big smile, showing her perfectly straight pearly whites.

"Well, hello, stranger. What brings you off the mountain?" she asked.

Willow Reid had made it known to Jake that in no uncertain words she would love to be with him on the mountain. Jake had known Willow for a number of years, and he and the other officers had eaten there often. Willow had been married in her younger years and at around 48 she was still a beautiful woman. Jake had been tempted a few times to ask her up on the mountain, but his love for Alona was still strong enough to deter him.

"Well," Jake said nervously, "I got to pick up some supplies and hog feed and get Wilson some treats."

"You know, Jake," Willow said in an amusing tone, "I don't understand how you can stay up there all alone with two dogs and some stray cats. It's a wonder you don't go stir crazy."

"Well, Willow," Jake replied, "you may be right. I've been having some strange things happen up there and I don't understand none of it."

Willow sat down across from him and he told her of what had taken place. She listened intently as he talked.

After Jake had finished, she said, "Well, it sounds scary, Jake. Do you think it's something to do with you being up there all alone and you're starting to see things?"

There was a smile on her face when she finished, and then she reached across the table and took his hand.

"You know," she said, "you need someone up there with you, and then you wouldn't be seeing and hearing things."

Jake smiled and replied, "Now, who in their right mind would want to live up there with an old man and an ugly dog?"

"Okay, Jake," she replied. "You're not old and Wilson is a cute dog."

"Well," he replied, "you haven't seen Dexter, either. He's a hound and his ears hang down to the ground and he sleeps all the time. And don't forget about the two hogs and all my chickens and my horse. "

"Wow," she replied, "sounds a lot like the farm where I grew up. And, yes, I love horses and would love to go riding again sometime."

"Well, Willow," he replied, "maybe sometime you can come up; and if you don't mind doubling, we can ride back behind the farm on some of the old logging roads."

"I would love to. When can we go?" Willow asked excitedly.

"Well, I've got hogs to kill and a lot of corn to get in yet ... and I still need to finish getting in my wood for the winter," Jake said.

"Well," she replied, "let me know."

They talked for a while longer, and after paying his bill Jake headed out to the feed store.

"Hello, Jake," Jerry Wilson said as Jake came through the door of Wilson's Feed and Seed. "What you need today?"

"Oh, some hog feed and cracked corn for the chickens," Jake replied. "I think I've got enough feed for the horse to last for a while."

Jake had always tried to keep enough feed ahead so his trips to town would be minimal.

After some small talk and loading the feed in the Jeep, which was now starting to show the load it was carrying, Jake headed out for his last stop at Mark's Convenience Store.

He had known Mark for some years and loved to listen to his English accent. Jake couldn't pronounce Mark's last name, so he always called him James Bond from the 007 movies.

Outside of Mark's store, Jake filled the Jeep up with gas and the two 5-gallon cans strapped to the back. As he was finishing up, his cell phone rang and the caller ID said "James Rose," Jake's son.

"Hi, Dad," James said over some awful music in the background. Jake hated the crap the young people listened to these days.

"Hello, Son," Jake replied. "How goes it up there at college?"

"Going good, Dad," James replied. "Another year I will be done."

"That sounds good," Jake replied. "Hope you learn how to work on those computers, Son."

"No, Dad," James replied, "I'm learning how to run them."

"Oh, sorry," Jake replied, "I forgot. So what you got on your mind?

"Well," Dad, "he replied," I was calling about you and Mom. You know, she's not going to sit out there and wait for you from now on."

"I know," Jake replied. "We've talked about marriage counseling, and I've agreed to go with her."

"Well, Dad," James replied, "you've said that before and you never went."

Jake loved to hear from his son, but hated when it was about him and Alona.

"Yes, I know," he replied, "but I'm going to try harder. Okay?"

"Well, you had better make it soon, before she decides to go out with Willy Hedrick. I know he's asked her, and she says she might go out with him."

Jake shuddered at the name of Willy Hedrick. Willy ran the store on Snowridge, next to where Jake and Alona had lived for the past 25 years. To Jake, Willy had always seemed to act like he was better than everyone else. In all probability, Willy could give Alona more than Jake could, but right now he didn't even want to hear Willy's name.

"Well, James," Jake replied, "that is something that your mom and I need to discuss. Okay?"

"Okay, Dad," James replied in an irritated tone. "Just don't want you to totally lose Mom."

After talking a few minutes, they hung up and Jake headed in to pay for his gas. The store was empty except for Mark and Tina Johnson, who worked for Mark. When she saw him, Tina flashed a quick smile and then resumed her chore of mopping the floor next to the cooler that held the ice cream and frozen pizzas. Mark was busy putting cigarettes in the rack behind the counter. He looked up as Jake came through the door.

"Hello, Jake," Mark said in his strong English accent. "How you been and how's everything on the hill?"

"Doing okay, I guess," Jake replied, not wanting to get into any conversation about the last two days.

Jake always picked up something sweet to eat at Mark's and he moved to the back of the store to locate some Honey Buns and chocolate doughnuts. As he was gathering up what he needed, he heard a voice coming from the front of the store and froze in his tracks.

Oh, God, he thought, *it can't be.*

After a few moments of listening he knew who it was, and from somewhere deep down inside he felt his anger start to rise.

Jake moved slowly down to where he could see the cash register and his suspicions were confirmed. There stood Stoolie Brown with his back to Jake. Stoolie Brown, whose real name was Steve Brown, had been the bully in school who picked on Jake and the other kids. He had earned the name "Stoolie" due to his telling on everybody and then daring them to do something about it. In school, Stoolie was a foot taller than Jake and outweighed him by at least 60 pounds. Over the years, Jake had reached 230 pounds and stood six foot five.

Jake stood listening to Stoolie talking to Mark. He still had the same obnoxious voice, and he was telling Mark about a big land deal that he had just closed. Mark looked back at Jake, and when he did Stoolie turned to face him.

"Well, well, well, if it isn't mama's boy Jake Rose!"

Jake stood for a few moments, then moved over to the counter to deposit his snacks for Mark to check him out and to pay for his gas. Stoolie stood about five and a half feet and he was still fat like he was in school. Stoolie moved within two feet of Jake and stood glaring at him the same way he would do when they were in school.

From somewhere Jake's right knee came up and caught Stoolie square in the groin. As Stoolie started back, Jake caught him with a roundhouse right that would have made Mike Tyson proud. Jake had gone through a lot of defensive tactics when he was a police officer and he was using every bit of it on Stoolie.

Somewhere to his left Jake heard Mark yelling to stop. Jake finished up on Stoolie with a left hook followed by another roundhouse right, which sent Stoolie backwards into a rack of bread, knocking it over. Jake started towards Stoolie, but before he could get to him Stoolie was up at amazing speed and almost took the door off its hinges and made a beeline to a gray Caddy in the parking lot.

Tina had called 9-1-1, and within minutes two police cruisers pulled up. Daryll McClain, the chief of police, and Jacob Trull came running in the store. Jake had started helping Mark pick up the loaves of bread that were scattered over the floor and putting them back on the rack.

"What's going on here?" Daryll asked. "We had a call that there was a fight, and we seen a Caddy going up Beech Creek at a high rate of speed. Another officer is trying to catch up with it. Jake, did you have anything to do with this?"

Daryll McClain had been the chief of police when Jake had worked in Judson as an officer, and they had always gotten along good, even after Jake had resigned his position on the force. Daryll looked over at Mark and asked him what had happened.

"Well, officer, some dude decided to take a swing at Jake here and he seemed to have fallen into my bread rack, and then he tore out of here like a bat out of hell. Don't really know what his problem was, officer."

Daryll turned and said, "Jake, do you know anything about this supposed fight?"

"Just like Mark said, Daryll; that seems to be the way it happened."

"Who was this guy, Jake?" Daryll demanded.

"Well, Daryll, do you remember Stoolie Brown?"

"Oh, hell, yes, I remember him. He used to pick on all the kids smaller than him and tell on everybody."

"Yep," Jake replied, "that's him."

Daryll looked down at Jake's hand and saw the blood on his knuckles and looked up at Jake with a smile.

"Well, hope that done some good. I think maybe Stoolie will think twice the next time he decides to be an asshole."

There were things that Stoolie had done to Jake that no one knew about, and Jake had made a vow to himself to never divulge that to anyone, not even Judy Grasson, even though Jake knew that it needed to be talked about.

As soon as Chief McClain pulled away, Jake said his good-byes, picked up his bags and hopped in the Jeep. As the old Willys purred along up Rocky Creek, Jake was lost in thought about what had happened at Mark's Convenience Store and how, after all these years, he had finally put Stoolie Brown in his place. His knuckles hurt and he knew they would be sore tomorrow, but he figured that pain would be gain, and for the first time in a while he felt good about himself.

Rocky Creek Church sat on a hill overlooking a great meadow, and on a portion of the hill was the graveyard where his mom was buried. As Jake approached the church, he could see the tombstone that marked the grave of Anella Blake. Jake hadn't been to her grave for some time, even though after she died he would feel guilty if he didn't visit it at least once a week. He pulled the old Willys into the parking lot and sat thinking about whether or not to walk up to the grave. He remembered, after she died, how he had spent hours there trying to find answers to so many questions and finally realizing the answers he was searching for lie within himself. There were things in Jake's past that had plagued him for years, and so many of them he couldn't remember.

Jake walked up the path with Wilson following close behind. He stood at the grave and read the inscription on the small stone that had been donated by the church: "Anella Blake born Jan 31, 1919 laid to rest July 20, 1988." A dove was cut in the stone on the bottom, with the inscription "Asleep in Jesus."

Jake sat down on the ground next to the grave, his thoughts going back to the few good memories he had as a child. He remembered when she would take him hunting for the food the Cherokees had used for many years, way before the white people had invaded their land. They had hunted "Wishy," a food the white man called "Hen of the Woods." There were also "Slicks" and "Water Creasy." She had shown him the mushrooms that could be eaten. There were roots from certain plants, such as Yellow Root, that were used for a medicine. As a child, Jake had seen her make baskets from the White Oak and from river cane. He remembered, on one occasion, going with her and his dad on a picnic up a beautiful valley that ran adjacent to Rocky Creek. It was one of the few times he could remember all three of them being together and they both seemed happy at the time.

As time went by, Jake had seen his mom go downhill. And when his dad died in 1966, it seemed like things really went all to hell. Her drinking and the men that woke him up in the middle of the night had made Jake hate her. It wasn't until after her death and what his aunt had told him that he was able to even begin to forgive her. His aunt had told him of the time Anella was raped, and that Jake had a half-sister out there that was a result of that rape. She also told him of the nervous breakdown his mother had had and how she had spent time in a mental hospital.

Jake sat at the grave for a while longer, and after collecting Wilson they headed for home. He passed a cornfield just before the road that led up to the mountain, and just on the other side of it was the "baptizin' hole," a place where the kids used to go swimming and was also used by the church when they did baptisms. Jake pulled to the side of the road and made his way through the cornfield until he was standing on the bank of Rocky Creek.

The place had been taken over by small trees and brush, but he could still see the big rock that they would jump off of when they were swimming. He thought of how, in the wintertime, they would dare each other to jump in the icy water. Jake stood thinking of how he seemed to remember more about the place, but nothing would ever really come into focus. Something happened here, he thought, and whatever it was must have been really bad, for him not to remember what it was.

As he stood thinking, he couldn't help but see something off to his left. He jerked his head in that direction hoping it was somebody fishing and they had walked up on him. He stared at the creek where the laurel was heavy and tried to make out what he had seen. Again he felt a chill run up his spine and thought of last night and how scared he had been. Then another movement just up the creek caught his attention. This time Jake was looking straight at it. He stared intently at the spot, and then he saw it, a face – or was it? The heavy laurel blocked most of the sun and he had trouble making it out.

Oh my God, he thought. *It can't be.*

The face had taken more shape, and just before it vanished he saw her. Jake had to hold himself together and suppress the strong desire to run back through the cornfield. A big part of him was trying to deny the fact that the face had been his mom's. He stood riveted to the spot trying to see the face again, but the laurel was the only thing moving as the water rushed by it.

Jake sat in the Jeep still reeling from what had just happened. "Was I imagining what I saw or is something trying to tell me something?" he asked himself.

The face Jake had seen, or thought he had seen, was of his mom from long ago. She had been a beautiful woman in her younger days and the face closely resembled a picture Jake had hanging over the fireplace in his cabin. Soon it was getting to be too much and he was really starting to wonder where reality and thinking you had seen something started. He sat in the Jeep for a few more minutes staring through the cornfield, hoping to see something that would prove he was wrong about the face he had seen. If only someone with a fishing pole would come into view to explain what he had seen. But the only thing that was moving was the breeze that slowly moved the leaves on the corn.

"There has to be some explanation for this," Jake thought as he fired the Jeep up and turned into the road leading up the mountain.

Jake had heard Alona's uncle, Larson Bearmeat, talk about the spirit that roamed the mountains. And up till now he hadn't put much faith in the stories, but with everything that had been happening he was almost ready to consider anything.

Larson Bearmeat lived on Slay Bacon Mountain, which had gotten its name from a pig farmer who had lived there many years ago. Jake had always liked Larson and always thought that he looked like a true Cherokee, with his dark brown weathered face and his gray hair that he'd keep in a ponytail that almost reached his midsection. Larson had helped Jake kill and dress out hogs in the past, and he knew that he was going to have to call upon him to help with the two hogs he had now. Larson lived alone in a small house that Jake had helped him build. His wife had died many years ago and they had never had any children. It was about eight miles to where Larson lived, and sometimes Jake would ride Commander around the mountain to go see him.

As Jake made the trip up the mountain to his cabin, he was starting to dread getting home, something that in a hundred years he would never have dreamed of.

Dexter was sitting in the road just below the cabin, and Jake had to blow the horn to get him to move. This was not like the dog that was most of the time sleeping on either the front or back porch. A thought crossed Jake's mind. It was almost like the dog was trying to stop him from going up the road.

Jake got out of the Jeep and lifted Dexter into the front seat with Wilson, but as soon as Jake moved back to the driver side, Dexter jumped out and moved back in front of the Jeep.

"Dexter," Jake yelled, "get out of the road."

Finally, after lifting Dexter back up into the seat and tying him up with a small rope he kept in the Jeep, he was able to continue on toward the cabin.

As Jake pulled into the yard and backed up to the building where he kept the hog feed, he had a sense of uneasiness as if something was wrong. After putting the feed away and giving some to the hogs, he pulled back into yard to take the supplies in the house. Everything looked okay, as Jake checked the house and even went upstairs to his bedroom. Still, he felt uneasy and couldn't really say why.

After attending to his usual chores, he walked to the edge of the yard and made a startling discovery. All of the chickens were gone. He checked the lot and found no evidence that anything major had happened to them, no feathers or anything. It was like they had all disappeared. There was still no sign of the cats, which was strange because they were usually on the back porch looking for something to eat. Dexter still sat in the front seat of the Jeep, even after Jake had removed his leash. After some coaxing, Jake finally persuaded the dog out of the Jeep.

Jake was starting to get jumpy and every little noise he would hear made him even more leery. Evening was coming on and he wasn't even sure he wanted to spend another night like last night on the mountain.

"Oh, crap, Jake, get ahold of yourself," he said out loud and turned and stomped off to go feed the horse. *You're a grown man, son,* he thought to himself. *Are you going to be scared away from your own home?*

Jake finished his supper, and after cleaning up the kitchen table he found enough scraps to feed Dexter. Dexter's house was on the edge of the yard. When Jake came out to feed him, he felt something was not right. The light on the porch cast a yellow glow in the yard, but the light fell short of Dexter's house and Jake had to venture farther to deposit the scraps in Dexter's bowl. Wilson had chosen to stay inside and devour the food that Jake had put in his bowl.

Jake bent down and petted Dexter as he filled his food pan. When he stood back up, he felt the hairs stand up on his neck and felt a chill run through every bone in his body. He felt riveted to the ground as if some unseen force had taken control of his ability to move.

Jake stood motionless for what seemed like hours and almost afraid to try and move. "What the heck," Jake said under his breath. He could feel a presence around him, and he desperately wanted to make a run for the front porch but chose otherwise. Something was there, and whether it wanted to harm him or not, it was scaring the crap out of him. He could feel his heart beating so loud that it had to sound like a herd of wild horses stampeding across the open plains.

Jake tried to see from left to right without moving his head, but couldn't detect any movement on either side. He made an attempt to shift his weight to try and see what was farther to his left. His legs felt like they weighed a ton. After some time, he managed to turn to where he could see the cabin out of his left eye. Terror gripped him like a vise and he wasn't sure if he had the strength to make it back to the front porch. Something moved just off the porch and Jake felt his breath sucked in like a vacuum. He stared intently trying to make out what he had seen, but the moonlight failed to illuminate anything.

The moon cast its pale light over the yard and shadows loomed like eerie spirits ready to consume whatever dared to invade their presence.

A breeze picked up like earlier in the day and suddenly he was shivering. Jake thought, *Whatever this is, it's scaring the shit out of me,* and knew he had to get back inside as soon as he could.

Something brushed by Jake, and with every ounce of strength he had he bounded across the yard to the porch and tore open the front door, almost ripping it from its hinges, and slammed it hard behind him. He fell back against the closed door and slid down until he was sitting on the floor as if to hold the door shut to whatever was out there. He sat there trying to regain his composure and noticed that Wilson was in the far corner staring at him with the hair standing up on his back. Jake spoke to Wilson, but he remained still, almost like he was in a trance. Jake managed to stand and retrieve his 12-gauge from over the fireplace and dropped double-aught buckshot in its chamber. Jake wasn't sure if the gun would do any good on what was outside. Hell, Jake wasn't sure about anything anymore.

As the night closed in and Jake set about cooking supper, his thoughts were upon the baptizin' hole and what he had seen, or what he thought he had seen. Now, after all these years with his mom being gone, how, out of the blue, had he seen her face in a laurel thicket? It didn't make any sense. Hell, the past few days hadn't made any sense. He was even considering the idea that someone was trying to scare the crap out of him. But who? He thought back to his time on the police department and tried to remember anyone that would have that kind of a grudge against him. Most of the things he had worked were drunk drivers and mediocre stuff. No one came to mind, and after putting that theory away he thought of what Larson Bearmeat had said about the spirits that roamed these mountains. Could he have done something here to disrupt something he wasn't even aware of?

Well, Jake thought, *I may have to ride over to Mr. Bearmeat's and have a talk with him.*

Chapter 3

The temperature had dropped during the night and Jake knew the winter was almost upon him. The cold weather had always been tough on him and seemed to make the depression worse, even with the medicine he was taking. He had learned over the years dealing with depression that in the winter months, when everything is dreary and cold and everything outside looks dead, it seems to intensify the depression. Somehow he had made it through the last few years on the mountain by chopping wood and staying busy, and some days he had just sat around the fire and tried to read. He knew that exercise helped, and a lot of times he would try and do strenuous chores until his back was hurting and he was eating pain pills like they were candy. At 56 years old, it didn't take a lot to put him in the rocking chair on the porch.

Jake could really feel the fight with Stoolie Brown and, as he figured, his knuckles were sore and, for whatever reason, his right leg was bothering him. But it was worth it seeing Stoolie go flying into the bread rack. So far he hadn't heard anything from the police department, so he figured Stoolie hadn't filed any charges on him. There had to be something to say about taking back a part of your life that had been marred by the likes of Stoolie Brown. There was still that thing with Stoolie that Jake couldn't think of right now.

Maybe later, he thought as he headed out the door to go feed the hogs and the horse.

There was still no sign of either the chickens or the cats. Jake stood in the doorway of the barn overlooking the cabin and he thought about what Glenn James had said about something not being right about the place. Jake remembered the log that had slid off the top and how he had been sure that it was scooted. There was something else that Jake had dismissed without much thought. One summer, when he was building the cabin and had gotten the roof on, he and Alona and James had camped out on the upstairs part. He had woken up to a sound that sounded like the moan he had heard earlier on the trail. The moan was just loud enough for Jake to hear and he had dismissed it as the wind blowing through the gable ends of the cabin. The more he thought about that night, the more he believed it was the same voice.

Jake found the number to Judy Grasson's office, and after speaking with the receptionist he had an appointment for Friday at 2 p.m. *That was quick*, Jake thought. Usually it took a couple of weeks to get in to see her. He knew deep down that he needed to talk to her about what had happened, especially him seeing his mom's face at the swimming hole and the things they had been working on before she had moved away.

Chapter 4

Judy Grasson's office was more like someone's living room minus the TV. She had greeted him with a hug and a lot of questions about what he had been doing since they had last met as counselor and patient.

She was a beautiful woman in her late 40s, with shoulder length auburn hair and a figure of a teenager. She had been through some traumatic events in her life and related well to what Jake had told her. She hadn't just been Jake's counselor, she had been his friend. He had even done some work around her house, which would probably be viewed by her coworkers as unprofessional. She had been one of the best counselors that Jake had been to, other than Tom Hollbrook.

They talked for a while before Jake started telling her what had been happening on the mountain in the past days. When he got to the part of seeing his mother's face at the creek, she stopped him.

"Jake, do you think that she could be trying to tell you something?"

"I don't know," Jake replied and added, "The face looked like one from a long time ago when she seemed happy at the moment."

"You know, Jake," Judy said, "we have talked about a lot of things that have taken place there. And I know there are still things that happened there that you can't remember. Do you think the face of your mom may be trying to tell you that you don't have to remember any of that? I know you have spent a large part of your life trying to undo what happened a long time ago. And I really think, deep down, you know that will never happen. So don't you think it's time to let that go and try to live your life without all the hatred you have for the person, or persons, that made it a living hell a long time ago?"

Jake told Judy about his altercation with Stoolie Brown and how, after all these years, he seemed to have put a part of his past behind him.

"How do you feel about this, Jake?" she asked.

"Well," he replied, "Stoolie was mean to me when we were in school; and when he shoved me in the stall in the bathroom and tried to pull my pants down, it done something to me. During the fight with him in the store, I think I was finally able to let go of that. Especially when I saw him go sprawling into the bread rack and hit the floor, for the first time in my life I wasn't scared of him anymore."

"You know, Jake, you proved, when you put on that police uniform, that you have come a long way from that little child. And I believe that you can beat this. It will be hard, as you know. But with my help and the medicine, I believe you can emerge from this victorious."

"Well," Jake replied, "I know I've come a long way, but sometimes I feel like I've wasted most of my life with this on my back and remember I'm 56 years old and can't handle the stress like I used to."

"You know, Jake," she replied, "you have accomplished a lot of things, like building your cabin, and you have a lot of skills that other people don't have."

"Yeah, I know," Jake replied. "But the price I've paid for it seems a lot more than I know how to do. And remember all those years of not being able to hang on to a job and having to depend on someone else most of this time to support me, that, in itself, is so depressing that a lot of times I wanted to kill myself. Judy, you don't know how hard it was for me to stay with the police department those years. Many a time I have sat looking down the barrel of my service weapon trying to pull the trigger. I think the wreck I had that night may have been a blessing in disguise. At least I know now that my disability check will come once a month and help my wife with the bills and I feel like at least I'm contributing something. It's true, I spent some of it to live on the mountain, but at least up there I can grow most of what I eat and there will be money from one of the hogs when I butcher them, along with the eggs I sell to a few neighbors – or did sell before all my chickens got gone."

"Jake," Judy asked, "can you stop for a minute and consider the possibility, though it may seem like a far reach, that all these things that are happening up there are something from your subconscious trying to tell you something?"

For a moment Jake felt his anger rise and thought, *How could she be saying that? Maybe I'm imagining all this.*

"No, Judy," his voice slightly raised, "this is real. My chickens left. My dog is acting strange. And I damn sure didn't imagine my cabin surrounded by what looked like a giant cloud. And, oh yeah, how would you explain my cell phone going crazy and my horse acting like he was going to break the door down in his stall? No, no, no. I may be a little crazy, but I'm far from imagining all this!"

"Sorry, Jake," Judy replied in a soft voice. "I had to see what your reaction would be to that question."

After a moment's pause, Judy asked, "Jake, do you have any idea what might be happening? Do you think someone from your days on the police department could be angry enough at you to do something like this?"

"No," Jake replied. "I've went over everyone I could think of and no one comes to mind. Judy, I know that in your line of work you probably wouldn't consider anything like spirits or ghosts or anything like that."

"Well," she replied, "I know there are a lot of things out there that can't be explained."

"Well," Jake continued, "I know an old Indian man, Larson Bearmeat, who lives on Slay Bacon Mountain; that is Alona's uncle who talks about restless spirits and spirits that have lost loved ones that walk the mountain in search of the ones they have lost. He is also a Cherokee medicine man and he has helped me before when I have killed hogs and beef. And I'm going to have to talk with him as soon as I can and see if he can shed any light on what's been happening. It's almost time to kill the hogs and maybe, with his Indian medicine, he can help me."

The time had slipped away, and after making another appointment with Judy he headed to town to make a quick stop at the public library to check and see if there was any kind of record or book as to where the Indian burial grounds were located around Judson. He found only one place, which was across town, and nothing even close to Rocky Creek.

Chapter 5

Jake spent most of the day gathering corn from the field. After shucking it and filling the corn crib to the halfway point, he made a trip to the upper field and gathered three containers of black walnuts. He loved to sit on the hearth in front of the fireplace and crack them like he had done as a child in the old house.

He sat under the giant walnut tree watching a squirrel carrying the walnuts to where it had made its home for the winter. With the thoughts of winter coming on, he could feel the depression coming on as well. What lay within him was kept at bay with the drugs, but even they sometimes failed when the world was dark and bleak.

It had been some time since he had thought about taking his own life, and he sometimes wished for a dreadful disease to take him over. If that ever happened, at least he would know that an end to all the crap in his life would come soon. He never had a death wish, but when the depression came down on him like a giant river, it would push him to the point of doing something drastic.

I guess I'm pretty strong, he thought, *to have gone through all these years and still be walking around.*

His thoughts were interrupted by Wilson standing underneath a White Oak tree barking at a squirrel that he had chased up it.

Jake loaded the walnuts in the old Jeep and headed back in the direction of the cabin. When he rounded the curve to where he could see the cabin, his heart jumped and for an instant he thought it was on fire. A haze hung in the air like the fog hangs over a valley, resembling a small lake. Jake goosed the old Willys to a speed where he was having trouble keeping it on the narrow road. As he drew closer, he could tell the haze was constrained to the area surrounding the cabin and the barn.

He slowed to a stop just before the barn and got out of the Jeep and stood looking toward the cabin. The haze had engulfed the cabin and it was hard to make out the chimney. He stood for a few minutes really unsure whether he wanted to venture any closer. Where he stood, he could tell the temperature had dropped at least 10 or 15 degrees. He turned back to the Jeep to see Wilson standing on the front seat with his paws on the dash looking intently toward the cabin. There was no sign of Dexter, and Jake thought about the first thing that he had experienced on the trail and how at that time it hadn't affected the old dog. *What has changed*, he thought, *to make the old dog try and block the road on my trip back from town? Is something trying to tell him something?*

Jake's disbelief in the tales he had heard from Larson Bearmeat was somehow starting to change. If he opened up to the possibility of ghosts, then maybe his mom's face was trying to tell him something. He thought of the face beneath the laurel and something occurred to him that he had failed to notice before. The look on her face held an expression that he remembered as a child when he had had a bad dream and she had held him and told him everything was going to be okay. But why now, after all these years? Nothing had ever happened remotely involving her.

Jake stood for a few more minutes and slowly started toward the cabin. As he entered the haze, he could feel the dampness surrounding him. He shivered wishing he had gotten his jacket out of the Jeep. As he neared the back porch, he knew that something was happening around him and he had an idea what it was about. Fear gripped him as he walked up on the back porch. He glanced back at the Jeep, which was just barely visible through the haze.

The back door stood eight feet away, glaring ominously at him like a door he feared would open up at the gates of hell. His imagination was starting to run wild and he desperately tried to get a grip on it. He glanced around expecting to see some hideous creature waiting to tear the flesh from his bones, but nothing was there, just the dark gray mist that surrounded him like a blanket on a cold winter day. He stood still trying to tell himself that whatever this was, it wasn't going to scare him off the porch. *Yeah, right,* he thought.

He stood for what seemed like hours, then finally took a step toward the back door. His clothes felt wet from the moisture, and then he realized that he was sweating. A large drop of perspiration ran down his forehead and into his eye. He wiped the sweat away, finding it hard to believe anyone could sweat in the cold. The silence was broken by his cell phone, and he jumped back as if a mad hornet had stung him on his butt.

"Shit!" he said aloud and flipped the phone open to see who was calling. The caller ID was a blur and the phone kept ringing even after he flipped it open and the ring tone, which was a song by Hank Williams, was distorted beyond recognition. Jake threw the phone into the backyard as he made a hasty retreat off the porch, and it lay in the yard still ringing. Hank Junior's voice sounded like something out of a horror show.

As Jake stood in the backyard a safe distance from the cabin, he heard the moan again. It sounded different than before, and even with Jake's diminished hearing the sound was deafening. He ran back to the Jeep, to where the haze hadn't reached yet, and after a few deep breaths attempted to undertake the process of getting his heart back to normal, which had been beating like the drums at a powwow. Wilson had retreated to the floorboard of the Jeep and was cowering down as if he was going to get hit at any moment.

Jake checked on the horse and found him at the back of the stable, his eyes big as saucers and ears laid back on his head. Jake could see he was trembling, and it looked like he might charge Jake at any time.

"Whoa, boy," Jake said. "What's wrong, fella?"

The horse calmed some at the sound of Jake's voice but remained at the back of the stall. Jake kept his distance and kept talking to him in an attempt to calm him down. After a few minutes of talking, the horse slowly came to Jake. He still seemed skittish, so Jake left the stall door shut for the fear that he might get spooked and run over him.

Jake stood in the doorway of the barn looking down at the cabin. Over the time that he was in the barn, the cloud had lifted some and was seeming to dissipate. His phone still lay in the yard but was quiet. Jake moved slowly down by the hog pen, and both hogs were asleep as if nothing had happened. As he approached the yard, he retrieved his phone, which appeared to be working in spite of Jake throwing it across the yard.

He stood in the yard surveying everything and noticed that Dexter had appeared from some unknown place. The old dog stood and looked at the cabin with his ears raised as if he sensed something. Then he walked across the yard and flopped down in his favorite spot where Jake had thrown an old jacket. For a few moments longer Jake stood in the yard before making his way back to the porch and walking to the door that before had seemed like his worst nightmare. He wasn't sure what he would find in the cabin, but slowly he pushed open the door.

The hinges creaked as Jake pushed open the door, this sound adding to his already elevated fear. As he pushed the door in and then took two steps back, a cold gust of wind blew by him like an escaping force freed from a tomb deep inside the earth. Jake could feel the dampness as the wind blew by him and he pulled his shirt closer to his body in an effort to keep from shaking. What he could see on the porch told him whatever had been in there had been released when he opened the door. He stood for a few moments longer before walking across the porch to stand in the doorway.

The inside of the cabin looked pretty much the way it did when he had left it earlier, other than the heavy coat of moisture that had been left by the change in temperature. The dampness hung in the air like smoke from a fire on a cold day. Nothing visible on the inside. After several minutes, Jake kindled a fire in the fireplace in an attempt to warm the cabin up and dry out the dampness that seemed to be on everything.

After he had gotten the fire going, Jake went back to where he had left the Jeep. All evidence of the mist was gone and Wilson was sleeping soundly on the front seat. Jake unloaded the walnuts and spent a good bit of time rolling them under his feet to remove the outer shell that was saturated with juice that was almost impossible to clean from your hands. Jake had seen the Indians use this to stain the White Oak when they were making baskets. With all the thoughts of what had happened earlier, he found it difficult to do the usual chores that he performed on a daily basis.

I've really got to go talk to Larson Bearmeat, he thought, and see if he can give me any idea of what is happening, before all this crap drives me crazier than I am already.

Chapter 6

The voice sounded distant and it held an echo that made it sound like it was coming from somewhere deep in Jake's mind.

"Hey, Jake, come over here, boy." The voice had a familiar ring to it and somewhere Jake could hear the sound of water as it made its way over the rocks in a downward spiral. Other voices sounded echoed from somewhere else, ones that Jake struggled to make out the identity of the persons that were speaking to him.

"Come here, boy," the first voice said again, but now in a whisper and sounded so close that Jake almost felt the breath that uttered the noise.

"Jake! You said you wanted to be our friend."

Jake struggled to understand who was speaking and where he was at. A familiar smell was in the air, one that Jake knew, and from somewhere deep inside he remembered where he knew it from. It was a combination of pine needles and wet decaying leaves. He could feel the terror rising from somewhere deep within him.

"No! No!" He tried to scream, but his voice only came out as a whimper. "No, please don't."

He tried to shout and felt a hand placed over his mouth as he felt himself being forced down on the ground where the strong smell of pine needles and decaying leaves filled his nostrils and he felt himself choking as he gasped for air.

The upstairs bedroom had a low ceiling, and Jake felt his head slam into it as he came out of the bed gasping for air. The jar was enough to send him back in the bed, and he rolled off into the floor with a thud. His breath was coming in gasps and he could feel his heart beating so loud that he thought it might explode from its place in his chest.

"Oh God," he sobbed, as everything he couldn't remember at the swimming hole came flooding out like a giant river on its way in search of the ocean. The many cigarettes over his life were telling on him as he started coughing uncontrollably and his fear rose even more at the thought of not being able to breathe.

"Oh my God!" he kept saying over and over as the tears streamed down his face like a waterfall. "Oh, my God!" this time saying it in his mind as if to elevate some of the things that he was now realizing had happened to him many years ago and had been locked up in the darkest regions of his mind.

Jake lay in the floor and slowly pulled himself into the fetal position, his arms trying to wrap around his body in an attempt to comfort the small child that Jake had become. He lay in this position for what seemed like hours almost afraid to move, as if the nightmare would start all over. Slowly the memories came into focus and he knew where all of this had taken place, and now he knew who the voices belonged to. Deep down, he could feel the anger starting to rise. His fear of them was now leaving and from his soul the vengeance to do something was slowly taking control of him.

He thought back to the day and how, after it was over, they had threatened to kill him if he spoke to a soul about what had happened. Now his adult life had taken that fear and turned it into a fiery rage that he felt could only be quenched by blowing their fucking brains from within the confines of their skulls.

Jake slowly rose from the floor and made his way down the stairs and retrieved his shotgun from its place over the fireplace. He grabbed his hunting vest and filled each elastic ring with double-aught buckshot. A glance at the clock showed 3:45 a.m., and he knew at this time they would probably be in their beds sleeping as if nothing had ever happened and with no remorse as to what they had done to a small child.

He grabbed his hat from the peg next to the door and flipped on the porch light and headed for the old Willys Jeep. The night was cold and the old Jeep spit and sputtered as Jake slung it into gear and headed down the mountain.

"Damn them," he kept saying as the old Jeep bounced over rock after rock. The old Cherokee Long Tom shotgun lay on the seat beside him, as if also on a mission to make a terrible wrong right. The headlights on the Jeep seemed to be in search of a predator as they covered the ground in front of the Jeep.

As Jake neared the entrance to Rocky Creek, he forgot the gate that he always shut each time he would head up the mountain. The Jeep slammed into the gate that Jake had built and the lower bar took out his right headlight as the gate gave way to the tremendous force of the Jeep. Jake had to duck down as the top of the gate came over the hood, shattering the windshield, spraying glass over Jake as he felt the blood from a cut over his eye running down his face.

"Damn it!" he shouted as the Jeep slid on the rocky road and almost went over the bank into Rocky Creek.

Jake regained control of the Jeep and pointed it down the road to where he knew his vengeance would take him. As he sped by the cornfield that he had earlier walked to, he looked towards the swimming hole, and what he saw caused him to lock the brakes on the Jeep and bring it to a screeching halt.

At first he thought there was a campfire at the swimming hole that was illuminating the trees that rose above where he had swum as a child. He sat in the Jeep staring at the light that deep down he knew was no fire. He held the old shotgun in his hands so tightly that they were beginning to cramp. Without moving the old Jeep from where he had stopped in the road, Jake grabbed the flashlight he kept in the Jeep and slowly started through the cornfield. Whatever this was had momentarily turned him away from what he had set out to do.

With each step Jake took, there was a new terror taking the place of the anger he had felt earlier. The closer he got, he could tell the light had no one certain place of origin, as if it was everywhere.

As he neared the bank that went down to the creek, he could see the entire swimming hole was illuminated and the light seemed to be focused towards the laurel that hung over the water where he had seen his mom's face. Jake walked to the edge of the water, the shotgun held tightly in front of him as if in an attempt to show whatever this was that he would shoot if necessary. He stood at the bank looking into the water, which resembled a swimming pool with lights at the bottom. Even though the night was cold, he could feel warmth coming from the water. And then he saw it, the face of his mom was again under the overhanging laurel, only this time her face was clear. It was the same face as before, the one Jake recognized from an old hand-painted picture that he kept on the mantle above the fireplace.

Jake went to his knees letting the shotgun fall by his side and felt the tears starting to well in his eyes.

"Oh God," he wailed as a voice rose above the water, a voice Jake knew well he had heard as a child when she held him close to her bosom and dried his tears when he had fallen off the mule and broken his leg.

"Jake, my son," she spoke with a voice that brought the tears flowing down his cheek and sobs that seemed to shake the ground where his knees were planted. "I'm so sorry, son, that your life had to be the way it is. I have been by your side in those times when you didn't feel like you could go on. Jake, my love for you has carried through all these years that I have been away from you. You are so much stronger than you think and you have lasted longer than most could have with the burden you carry. And it's time, Jake, to let all of it go."

"I sent the dream, Jake, so you could remember what happened at this place and you could start to heal – it will do no good to go and do harm to the ones that did this awful thing to you. Jake, if you do that, it will only bring pain and suffering to the ones around you that love you. I wouldn't have brought the dream to you if I didn't know you were strong enough to handle it. Jake, the mountain can only hold pain and suffering for you, for there is something up there I can't help you with. Sell this place, Jake, and move far away before it's too late."

Slowly the light around the laurel started to dim and the face of his mom was consumed by darkness as the flashlight Jake held cast an eerie beam over the water stopping on the big rock that Jake and the kids used to jump off of.

Chapter 7

Jake sat on the bank of Rocky Creek for what seemed like hours, and from somewhere in the distance he heard an owl hoot. The Cherokees believe that that is a sign that someone is going to die in the near future. How ironic, Jake thought, especially after what he had just witnessed.

He made his way back through the cornfield to the waiting Jeep. He had left the headlights on and the one light cast a yellow glow through the trees that stood at the end of the cornfield. The battery had passed the point of starting the old Jeep. After pushing it off the hill that led by the cornfield, it sputtered to life and Jake went as far as the church before turning around. He pulled in the parking lot of the church and sat looking at the church that was illuminated by the one light on the Jeep. He could remember, as a child, coming to church and how the preacher had seemed to always preach on the fires of hell and how everyone who wasn't "saved" would go there after they died.

He backed the Jeep up and pulled up the road to the graveyard. After parking the Jeep where it wouldn't roll off, he cut the engine and got out. Darkness hung over the graveyard and the only light he could see was from a house in the distance. With flashlight in hand, he walked to where his mom was buried. For some reason that he could not explain, the fact of being in a graveyard at night didn't scare him.

As Jake had left the swimming hole, he felt a sense of something being lifted from the burden he had carried all these years and had to admit it felt good. Jake sat down at the end of her grave and switched off the flashlight and the darkness settled around him. He sat in the quiet cool night with her headstone just barely visible, a headstone that had been donated by the church after her death. The anger in him had subsided and now he only felt tired. The jacket he had grabbed before leaving the cabin was warm, and he laid down with his head on the foot of the grave.

A noise in the background startled Jake awake and he sat up with a jolt. The sound had been a car on the road below the graveyard, and he realized the day was breaking into morning.

Goodness! he thought, *how could I have gone to sleep on the cold ground? And what time is it?*

He felt for his pocket watch and remembered that he had left it at the jewelry store on the trip to town. He stood up, trying to get the feeling back in his legs, and realized just how cold he was. The old Jeep sat silently waiting, and by the early morning light he could see the damage to it from crashing through the gate. The right front headlight was completely gone and in its place was a piece of wood that had before held his gate together. The windshield looked as if it had been hit with a load of buckshot from the shotgun that lay in the seat.

Jake touched his face and felt a large knot and dried blood and pulled back his hand when the pain shot through his head. After removing as much of the glass, and cutting his hand in the process, he rolled the old Jeep down the hill and headed for home.

Chapter 8

By the time Jake arrived at the cabin, his hands were numb and his feet felt like two blocks of ice. His back was hurting him ferociously from lying on the ground. After downing two painkillers, he proceeded to build a fire to ward off the coldness in the cabin.

Wilson met him at the door and jumped up on him in hopes of the treats that Jake kept in the kitchen cabinet. As the heat from his fire slowly filled the cabin, Jake fixed a light breakfast. His appetite lately hadn't been much and he attributed it to all that had been going on in his life. He sat in the recliner next to the fireplace thinking about what had taken place earlier, and deep down he knew there was something here in this place and he desperately needed to know what it was.

The sun had brought the temperature up considerably and Jake knew it was time to go speak with Larson Bearmeat. Within a few minutes, he had the saddle on Commander and was on his way toward Slay Bacon Mountain.

The trail that took him to Slay Bacon Mountain passed through what Jake thought was the most beautiful place on earth. The trail wound around the mountain opposite Jake's cabin, and from one point he could see the cabin and the barn. Jake knew he could have taken the Jeep, but he felt that he needed this time to digest what had been the biggest event in Jake's 56 years of living on the earth.

He stopped under some giant oak trees at a spring that came from under the large moss-covered boulder. After making a small dam in the branch so his horse could drink, he pulled a small packet from his saddlebags and sat on a rock eating a sandwich he had prepared before he left home. From where he sat, he could almost see to Judson.

The valley below was totally alive in the gray of autumn and the afternoon sun brought the red and yellow leaves to what looked like an Indian blanket Jake had once seen in a display at the Museum of the Cherokees. He sat in awe, taking in what was around him and silently wishing he could stay in this spot forever. Below him the giant oaks and hemlock moved in unison to the light breeze that was blowing their branches lifted toward heaven, as if in thanks for their privilege to adorn the mountains.

Over the trees, he could detect a smoke that he knew came from Cobb Lumber Company, that a lot of people in Judson depended on to make a living. To his far left he could see the massive towers that provided cell phone service in Judson. Jake felt for his phone and realized that he had left it in its charger in the cabin. *Oh crap,* he thought. It was too far to go back and get it, and he hadn't really felt like talking to anyone, so he took it as a blessing in disguise. The rest of the ride was uneventful, other than the deer he spooked from a cluster of small pines below the road.

Jake loved deer meat and the sight of one prompted him to make plans to go hunting later.

Larson Bearmeat's small house sat on a ridge overlooking the valley below. The road that led up to his house reminded Jake of his own road. Approaching the house, he passed an old Jeep that Larson had driven until it had stopped on the road refusing to go another foot. Two goats were tied up on the bank below the house in an effort to rid the hill of anything that grew, and they had done a pretty good job, only leaving the few rocks that protruded from the ground.

Larson was a pack rat and the two buildings below the house were overflowing with everything from old chainsaws to garden tools, and an array of cheap weed eaters hung on the wall, most of which had outlived their usefulness sometime ago.

As Jake passed the chicken house, two roosters were fighting and both seemed intent on becoming the winner. Three dogs lay sprawled in the yard, none of which Jake thought would ever leave the confines of the yard to dare chase a squirrel.

Larson Bearmeat sat in an old rocking chair on the porch, his head on his chest sleeping, his cowboy hat blocking the afternoon sun. He was a big man, probably even taller than Jake in his younger years. His gray hair fell almost the length of the red flannel shirt he had tucked in just above his belt. Alona had told Jake a lot about Larson and how, in the Vietnam War, he had saved his platoon by taking out four Vietnam soldiers with his bare hands and that he had received countless medals during his time in the Marines.

Jake sat on Commander a short distance from the porch before calling out in a voice that wouldn't startle the old man.

Larson spoke without raising his head, "Hello, White Man. You think you caught me asleep?"

Jake's Indian blood had never been enough to even start to make him resemble anything that remotely looked like a Cherokee and Larson had always referred to him as "White Man."

"What you doing on this side of the mountain?" Larson asked. "Time to kill those hogs?"

"Well," Jake replied, "there is something I need to talk to you about."

"Well," Larson replied, "come on up and sit on the porch and I will get us a cup of coffee."

Jake held the steaming cup of coffee and took a small swallow, which almost took his breath. Seeing this, Larson let out a laugh that seemed to carry to the valley below. Seeing the cut on Jake's face, Larson made a comment about Alona coming up on the mountain and beating the shit out of him with a piece of stove wood. Then he burst out laughing. Jake passed the cut on his face off as an accident that had happened when he was splitting wood. He didn't feel like explaining what had really made the cut and trying to tell Larson all the details that had transpired during the early hours of the day, and especially about him going to sleep on a grave. Larson would have probably said it was some restless spirit that he had offended, and part of that was probably right.

"Larson," Jake's voice capturing Larson's attention, "tell me again some of the stories about what is supposed to happen if some sacred place is violated and what would likely happen."

Larson studied Jake's face for a few moments before speaking.

"What makes you think that you have disturbed such a place?"

"Well," Jake replied, "I'm not sure I have, but there have been a lot of things happening around my place that I have no clue about."

Jake went on to explain what had happened on the trail and the experience he had when he went out to feed the dogs.

He also told Larson about the mist that had hung in the air around the cabin and included the part where his cell phone had gone crazy, how his chickens had left, and the way his horse was acting. Jake could see the expression change on Larson's face to a look that Jake had never seen before. The expression was like that of a very troubled person, and Jake even detected what looked like fear in the old man's eyes. Larson moved his gaze from Jake and sat staring down into the valley. After what seemed like hours, he turned back and faced Jake. When he spoke, there was almost a trembling in his voice.

"Jake, what you told me sounds like something I remember as a child. Many years ago, a white man came to this place with his family and built a small house on what is called Janson Ridge."

Jake knew this place well. He had hunted squirrels there with JJ and Benny Binion. It was located on the other side of the mountain from where Jake had built his cabin.

"Jake," Larson said, "I was told by the tribal members that there was an Indian burial ground on that mountain and it was considered a sacred place. Back then, the word of an Indian wasn't considered to be of any importance and Joshoway Jenkins, I think his name was, went ahead and built his home there. For a number of years nothing happened. One day, Joshoway come home to find all of his horses and cows and animals had vanished into the thin air. There was never any sign that someone had taken them, and the sheriff never found any evidence to prove otherwise. After that, things seemed to go downhill for Mr. Jenkins and he started telling wild tales about things that were happening around his place."

Jake felt a shiver go up his spine when Larson spoke of all the animals that had vanished and how the same thing had already taken place at Jake's home. He knew Larson's story would spell out the things to come, and Jake's fear rose even more with each word the old man spoke.

Larson paused as if the next words he chose would be his last. Jake studied the features of Larson's face trying to anticipate what horrors he might speak of. Larson took a deep breath and continued.

"For some time after the animals had vanished, nothing happened, until one day the sheriff made a visit to Josh Jenkins' home to check if there had been any news of his animals or if anything else had disappeared. He found Josh and Annie hanging from a rafter in their house. The sheriff said it was the most gruesome sight he had ever witnessed. Josh had strung two ropes from the rafters within one foot of each other and Josh and Annie, the sheriff said, were clinging to each other as if they were trying to comfort each other in the last seconds of their lives. He also said the look on both their faces were frozen in some unspeakable terror that they must have witnessed seconds before stepping off the kitchen table to their deaths.

"The sheriff said their two small children were found locked in a closet in the bedroom, as if Josh was attempting to protect them from whatever terror that had found its way into their home. The children were so scared that they could only babble about what had happened and, if I'm not mistaken, both of them had been in a mental hospital most of their lives. The sheriff said the inside of the house had a strong smell of mildew and everything in the house was damp."

Jake felt the fear cut through him like a sharp knife, as he recalled his cabin and the moisture on everything. Larson had paused and was looking intently at Jake. When their eyes met, Jake knew the old man was troubled. After a few moments, Jake told Larson what had taken place over the last weeks. The old man listened intently as Jake told him about the incident on the trail, and how he had found the cabin in the mist that hung over it like a cloud, and how his chickens had left, and how Wilson had been acting.

After Jake finished his story, Larson cast his gaze down the mountain and for a few moments said nothing. He turned back to Jake with the same worried face as before and spoke in a voice that held genuine concern.

"You know, Jake, you have got to leave that mountain before whatever is up there destroys you. I know you love that place and you worked hard building the cabin, but if you don't leave you may soon end up like Josh and Annie."

With that, Larson rose to his feet, grabbed Jake's coffee cup and went through the screen door, letting it slam behind him. The noise from the screen door made Jake jump and he stood up and walked to the edge of the porch and stood staring in the direction of where his cabin sat. Larson appeared on the porch with both cups full of hot coffee and stood beside Jake.

"Larson," Jake spoke as he took the steaming coffee from him and returned to his chair, "Alona has told me that you are a medicine man. Is that true?"

Larson smiled and took a swallow of the coffee before answering Jake's question.

"Well, Jake, I used to take part in the rituals of our tribe and I have learned some of the medicine man's ways, but it has been years since anyone has asked me that question."

"Well, Larson," Jake interrupted, "is there anything you could do to try and stop what is happening on my mountain?"

"Well, Jake, I'm not sure if my medicine would do any good against what you say is happening. And if there is something there that was strong enough to make two people hang themselves, it would take very strong medicine to fight this evil."

"Well, Larson, do you think that there is any chance that I may have built my cabin on an Indian burial ground?"

Before Larson could speak, Jake told him of stopping at the county library in search of any information that might indicate where the burial grounds are located.

"Larson, there wasn't much information about burial grounds except one location that is across town."

"Well, Jake," Larson spoke, "not a lot of records were kept back then, and most of the white people didn't think that our burial grounds were any more of importance than the Indians that lived here. No offense to you, White Man," Larson said with a half-smile.

"Well, Larson, would you be willing to at least try with your medicine?" Jake asked in a voice that sounded desperate. "You know, Larson, I don't want to go back to Snowridge, or anywhere else as far as that's concerned. This is the place where I grew up and it's taken me a long time to be able to stay there. I know Alona is your niece and you probably think that I should be out there ..."

"Whoa, Jake," Larson stopped him before he could continue. "You're right, Alona is my niece, but I learned a long time ago to keep out of other people's problems. Jake, I think you are a good person. And if you and Alona can't get along, then I will not put my opinion where it doesn't belong."

They stood silently on the porch before Larson spoke again.

"Jake, I will come to your place and do what I can with my medicine, but I can't promise you anything and I want you to understand that before I go. Okay?"

"Okay," Jake replied as a sense of hope arose and he instantly felt better even though he wasn't really sure if Larson could do any good.

Both men sat for some time talking about one thing or another. After Larson put some eggs from the henhouse in a small bag, he informed Jake that he would have to come and get him in the Jeep because he was too old to ride horseback around the trail.

Jake made his way back down the road to where the trail took off around the mountain, and within an hour he was taking the saddle off Commander and thinking about what he would fix for supper.

Chapter 9

The day following Jake's visit to Larson Bearmeat, he worked putting up corn and stocking the corn house with an array of canned corn, tomatoes, and apples from the orchard. He filled the hole in the bank below the cabin with potatoes, covering them in hay he had gotten for the horse. All that time Jake kept thinking about going to pick up Larson, but he could be stubborn and kept putting it off to the night that changed his mind drastically.

Jake had worked most of the day filling the woodshed to where it was overflowing, and to any person it would look like there was enough food to last 10 years. He had been tired from the day's work and had taken two painkillers after eating his supper. He watched TV for a while before retiring to his bed and a glance at the clock on his nightstand which read 9:25. It was a little early for him to be going to bed, but within minutes he was asleep with Wilson on the foot of the bed.

From somewhere in the distance, Jake could feel the cold, and there was a tightness that seemed to engulf him like a giant hand trying to squeeze the life out of him. His muscles seemed frozen and his breath was slowly being pushed out of him like a child squeezing the last bit of air from a balloon. He struggled to break free of the dream he thought he was having, and after finally getting his eyes to open he realized the ceiling of the cabin was just inches from his face. As he struggled to turn his face, he was confronted with the fact that he was awake and his bed was empty.

He felt a scream trying to find its way from inside his lungs, but no sound escaped when he opened his mouth. The sight of Wilson's disfigured body lying on the floor next to the bed was as if some creature in a murderous rage had torn the small dog apart like a lion devouring its newfound meal. Blood was splattered on the bed and Jake could see droplets clinging to the handrail that led down the stairs. A flood of grief and anger swept over him as he fought to break away from this sinister being that held him suspended like a giant chandelier in some rich family's home. The moisture around him seemed to penetrate through his skin and his bones felt the chill like the cold on a February morning.

From somewhere around him, a scream broke through that sounded like someone in medieval times that had been strapped to a vicious torture device and their bones were being pulled from their place. The sound was deafening and Jake wasn't really sure if he was hearing the scream or if it was coming from within him. Something flashed within his head and he felt the floor of the bedroom slam into him. Total darkness invaded him and what little breath he had in his lungs was knocked from them.

Jake felt something warm and wet against his face. Upon opening his eyes, he was face-to-face with Wilson's ugly mug. He sat up so fast that his focus on Wilson was lost and his head started spinning. Jake was in the floor of the bedroom and he could feel a pounding throb of pain shooting through his head. He felt the back of his head and discovered a large bump just above his left ear. He sat in the dim light of the bedroom for a few minutes holding Wilson close to him and saying a silent prayer that this had only been a dream.

Jake knew for certain now that what his mom had said was true and he had to do something quick. It was going to take a lot to drive him from this place and he was determined to do everything in his power to stay here. The clock showed 6:10 a.m. and there was no way he could go back to sleep. His fire had turned to glowing embers and a chill was in the air, but it was nothing compared to the chill he had felt in the dream.

Jake made a pot of coffee and sat in his recliner looking through the window at the valley below. The dream had seemed so real ... a little too real for him. From the bump on his head, he figured he must have rolled out of the bed and struck his head on the nightstand. He made his way back up the stairs to the bedroom and inspected the nightstand. Everything looked okay and the picture of the grandkids was sitting in its usual place undisturbed.

"If I hit the nightstand, wouldn't it have knocked the picture and the clock off?" he almost said out loud.

He stood looking at the ceiling and then he saw it, a blood splatter that traveled part way across the ceiling, stopping just about the foot of his bed. For a moment he stood staring at the red spots that covered the old tongue-and-groove pine that Jake had pulled from an old house on Snowridge that he had torn down for lumber when he was building his cabin. Slowly he reached up, touching the spot and feeling the sticky substance. He pulled his hand back quickly, as if he was bringing back part of the horror of his dream. He knew for sure now that the dream wasn't just in his head.

Jake stood looking at the blood on his hand and slowly brought it to his nose. The smell was disgusting and he jerked his head back. With his other hand, he examined the lump on his head hoping that there was blood in his hair to somehow explain what he was seeing. He ran his fingers through his hair frantically, but the only thing he found was the lump. He tried to place the smell of the blood, or whatever it was, and after a few minutes he knew where he had smelled it before.

When he was with the Judson police, he had been called to an old house in town. The house had been occupied by Lawrence Kenny and his neighbors were concerned that he hadn't been seen for at least a week. After some time, someone had come up with a key to the old house and Jake and two other officers had gone in to search for Mr. Kenny. In Mr. Kenny's bedroom, Jake had found him with a single shot to the head from a .22 rifle. The blood had pooled beside Mr. Kenny's head on the bed where he had ended his life. The coroner determined that he had been dead for at least six days, and the smell of the blood wasn't something that Jake had ever forgotten.

Jake stood in the small bedroom trying to examine every aspect of the dream. He moved to the top of the stairs and stood gazing down at the small living room. When the bouts of depression had overtaken him, he would sit in the recliner and survey everything in the cabin and sometimes, sitting there, he would feel better knowing what he was looking at was something he had built with his own hands.

The ceiling was 16-foot high, if you were standing in the living room, and the old chestnut log that ran the length of the ceiling and a few of the other logs were the only thing that Glenn James had helped him with. Jake had built everything in the cabin by himself, from the kitchen table to the end tables and the attic dresser that held his clothes. He had laid every rock that was in the fireplace and the chimney that towered above the highest point of the cabin.

The wood cook stove had come from an old house that Jake had torn down that had belonged to the Binion family. The old stove held a lot of memories that Jake cherished. They were memories of a happy family, and every time he cooked a meal on the old stove he could see Hazel Binion standing over it frying potatoes and stirring a pot of pinto beans. For some reason Jake could never get the beans to taste as good as the ones Hazel had cooked. As a child, the warming closets on the old stove had always seemed to be filled with leftovers that Jake would devour when he came visiting.

Jake sat staring in the fireplace watching the flames as they devoured the wood that he had placed there earlier. It had taken only a few minutes to clean the blood from the ceiling in the bedroom, and after making his bed he retreated back to his recliner. He now knew, without a doubt, that the line between fantasy and reality had been crossed, and this troubled him deeply. Try as he might, he could find no explanation for what had taken place in the early hours, and he desperately needed to find one. It seemed, now, that his home was becoming his most fearful enemy and his cabin was threatening to consume him. What once had been a comfort zone was now becoming his worst nightmare.

The silence in the cabin was broken by Jake's cell phone. Checking the caller ID, he cursed under his breath for, right now, Alona was the last person he wanted to talk to. He flipped the phone open and tried to speak in a tone that wouldn't reveal to Alona any indication that anything was wrong.

"Jake, what's going on up there? I saw Larson and he said you came to see him."

Her voice held a genuine concern that Jake had not heard in some time, and that, in itself, made him feel somewhat less agitated.

"Well, Alona, Jake responded," if you spoke to Larson, you should know why I went to see him."

"Well, Jake," she said, "he didn't tell me a lot, just that things were happening there and you had asked him to come over with his medicine."

"Well, Alona," Jake replied, "there have been things happening here. And the reason I haven't told you is, I thought you would start with all the stories about Skillies and the little people and that some dreaded spirit was trying to drive me insane."

With that statement to Alona, Jake suddenly realized that what he was saying could very well be true. There had been a point in time, with all this, that Jake had considered the possibility that he was losing his mind.

"No, Jake!" Alona said in a little louder voice, "I wasn't going to say anything like that. It's just that Larson seems to think that you have disturbed something that is sacred and he isn't sure if his medicine will help you."

"Well, Alona," Jake replied, "I really don't know what is happening up here, and I have no idea what to do other than to start believing all the stories that I've heard Larson tell. You know, Alona," Jake continued, "I seem to be dealing with two different things, the things that happened to me as a child and whatever the hell I've done here to upset some spirit that is dead set on driving me from this place."

"Well, Jake," Alona said in an inviting voice, "you could always come back here and live with me and the grandkids. Lord knows they miss you ... and I miss you, too."

Jake almost exploded with the idea that he would have to go back to Snowridge and live in Dawson Cove.

"Alona! No!" Jake said abruptly. "I will not be driven off this mountain by some spirit or whatever the hell it is that has taken up residency here."

The phone was silent for a few moments before Alona finally spoke again.

"Well, Jake, you know I'm not going to sit out here forever waiting on you to figure out what you want. Jake, I know you have so much weight on your shoulders from the thing that happened a long time ago, and I think it's about time that you let go of the pain you carry, because no matter what you do you can't change anything that happened back then. I know you built that cabin to try and recreate something from your past that was good. Jake, I love you and I want you to be happy, but I really don't believe that you're going to find it up there."

Her words ran through Jake like a chill, as he remembered what he had heard in the early morning on the creek bank when the voice of his mom had told him almost the same thing.

"Well, Alona," Jake replied in a more sober tone, "I still love you, but I don't really believe that there is happiness for me anywhere. I'm sorry that you have had to endure all these years with my problems and the many times that I have let you down. Sometimes I wonder what your life would have been like if I hadn't come along."

"Jake," Alona interrupted, "it was my choice to stay with you and I could have left at any time. Okay?"

"Yeah, I know," Jake replied, regretting what he had just said.

"You know," Alona continued, "there is truth to what the old people have said about disturbing a sacred place. And if you have, I hope that Larson's medicine is strong enough to put whatever it is back where it came from. Jake, did Larson tell you about the spirits that guard over the sacred places?"

"Well, no, he didn't," Jake replied, thinking that Larson had failed to tell him these things in case his medicine wasn't strong enough to protect him.

"Jake, the story I've heard as a child was that the spirits of the ones that were bad were doomed to protect the sacred ground for eternity and those spirits are very evil. If you have destroyed a sacred place, they will not stop until they drive you from this place or you are dead. Did Larson tell you the story about Joshua Jenkins and his wife?"

"Yes, he did, Alona, and I find that hard to believe, that some spirit can be strong enough to make two people hang themselves. It just doesn't make sense."

"Well, Jake," Alona replied, "it happened, and to this day nobody has been able to explain what really happened." After a short silence over the phone, Alona knew Jake just need her to listen to him and said, "Jake, tell me what's been happening up there."

Through the conversation between him and Alona, Jake decided to tell her everything that had taken place in the past weeks. He started with what took place on the trail and everything that had happened, including the dream earlier. The phone was silent, and when Alona spoke he could tell that she was crying.

"Oh, my God, Jake. That had to be really rough on you, especially at the creek and you sleeping on her grave. Jake," Alona now spoke in a voice that Jake could detect a sound of fear in, "I'm really worried about what you have told me and I wish you would leave that place before it's too late. I can't help but feel that something bad is going to happen."

"Hold on, Alona," Jake interrupted. "Nothing is going to happen to me. I'm going to be fine." That was something that Jake wasn't even sure of himself, and before he had even finished telling Alona that he was starting to have doubts himself, Alona interrupted him.

"There is someone else you could go see who knows a lot about the Indian burial grounds and where they are at. It's old man Will Hardy who lives on Teesateskie Road. I think he could tell you for sure where the burial grounds are at."

Jake didn't say anything as his thoughts wandered. Alona spoke up and said, "Jake, did you hear what I said?"

"Yeah, I heard you," Jake replied. "I guess that I will go see him. I need to know for sure where my cabin sits."

They talked for a while longer before hanging up. Jake sat for a while thinking, I hope this isn't a wild goose chase.

Chapter 10

Teesateskie Road laid just west of Upper Creek Road and as Jake turned the old Jeep on the road, he found himself remembering going up this road when he was a child. Jake's dad had brought him there when he would buy cornmeal from the Adams Grist Mill. Jake passed the remains of the old mill and remembered going in the mill with his dad and how loud the mill was as it ground the corn into cornmeal. It seemed like all the places that Jake had been as a child were gone.

As Jake drove the winding road, he was amazed at how many fancy houses dotted the mountainside. After a few more miles, Jake found himself at the end of the road and in front of Will Hardy's house. The house was small and a wisp of blue smoke escaped from the chimney. There were at least 30 chickens in the yard, and they scattered as Jake made his way up the small sidewalk that led to the house.

The porch was cluttered with rocking chairs and an ancient deep freezer that sounded like it was on its last effort to keep running. Jake made his way to the door and knocked on the wood screen door that was missing the top part of the screen. From inside Jake heard a dog bark and could hear someone moving toward the door.

"Who is it?" a voice said from behind the door.

"It's Jake Rose, Mr. Hardy. I was wondering if I might speak with you."

The door opened part way and a small man stood peering out.

"What do you want to talk about, son?" the old man asked.

"Well, sir," Jake said, "Larson Bearmeat said I might get some information from you."

The old man opened the door and pushed the screen door open.

"Did you say Larson Bearmeat sent you?"

"Yes. He told me you could give me some information about the Indian burial grounds that are located in the county."

"Well, come in," the old man said and stepped aside so Jake could come in.

Will Hardy was in his seventies and didn't look to weigh over 125 pounds. His old army jacket was well-worn and the hat he was wearing had long ago lost the logo. Jake could tell the old man had long ago stopped caring what he looked like. The gray stubble of a beard covered his leathery face, and when he spoke Jake noticed that all but a few teeth still remained with the old man.

"You say Larson sent you? I haven't seen him in a lot of years. How's he doing?"

Jake responded, "Well, he's doing okay, I guess, for his age. Still living on Slay Bacon Mountain with all his chickens."

The living room was just as cluttered as the porch, with old newspapers and a small potbellied stove in the corner of the room. Jake glanced in the kitchen where the sink held a mound of dirty dishes.

The old man said, "So you want to know about the Indian burial ground?"

"Yes," Jake replied.

The old man hesitated for a moment before speaking.

"You know, I think I have a map that shows where they're all at, if I can find it. And why do you want to know about them?"

Jake started telling the old man about where he had built his cabin and the things that had been happening in the past few weeks. The old man listened. And when Jake had finished, the old man moved to the desk that sat covered with old books and papers and pulled one of the drawers open and started looking through the papers.

Without looking up, he said, "So, did Larson tell you about the legend of the evil spirits that are placed around the burial grounds?"

"Well, yes, he did," Jake said. "I was hoping that my cabin wasn't built on one of those."

The old man continued to sort through the papers he had pulled from the drawer and finally pulled one yellowing paper from the others.

"Yes, here it is," he said as he took the paper across the room to a lamp.

Jake followed him, and the old man sat down on a worn recliner that had seen its better days.

"Let's see," the old man said. "Can you show me where your cabin is located?"

Jake found Upper Creek Road and pointed to where he thought his cabin was located. The old man put on his glasses and stared at the place where Jake had pointed.

"Well, son, you can see here, there is one burial ground located here," as he pointed at the exact spot where Jake had indicated.

Jake felt his heart skip a beat and for a moment he felt lightheaded.

"You know, son," the old man spoke, "I'm positive there is at least two burial grounds on that mountain, and there may be more than that."

Jake thought a moment before speaking. "Will," he said, "I've been having all kinds of problems up there." Jake began to tell the old man what had been happening, and when he finished the old man was silent for a few moments before he spoke.

"Son, there are a lot of things that I don't understand when it come to the Indian affairs. There are so many legends about the burial ground and what would happen if someone were to destroy one of them. I know of one legend about a small girl that haunts the mountain. They say she is searching for her grandmother and at times you can hear her cry. The legend goes that a long time ago, an old Indian lady left the village and went in the mountains to die. A short time after she left, her granddaughter left the village in search of her and no one from the village ever saw her again. Members of the village searched the mountains, but no trace of her was ever found. The legend goes that at times you could hear her cry in search for her grandmother."

Jake thought of the day on the trail and how he had heard something and wondered if what he had heard could possibly be what Will Hardy was referring to. All the talk about legends and spirits was starting to spook Jake and he knew he had to do something.

"Well, Will," Jake said, "is there anything I can do to rid these spirits from my cabin?"

"Well, Jake," Will said, "maybe Larson and his medicine can help you. And if he can't, there is only one thing I can think of and you're not going to like what I'm about to say. I've heard that the only way you can get rid of any spirits is to purge the land, and that means by fire. You would have to burn your cabin down and move off the mountain for good."

Just the thought of all the work he had put into building the cabin made Jake mad. And before one thought he cursed under his breath, "Hell, no!" He wasn't going to get run off that mountain by some restless spirits and a legend about a small girl hunting for her granny.

Will Hardy noticed the anger in Jake's face, and after a few moments he spoke up.

"Jake," he said, "the spirits are strong. And I don't know if you have heard the story about the family who built their house on what they knew was an Indian burial ground and the sheriff found both of them hanging in their house. Jake," he said, "you have to be careful when it comes to messing with something that you know little about. I wish there were something I could tell you to help. But I'm like you, I don't know enough about the spirit world to help you. I only hope that Larson's medicine will help. It will take some strong medicine, and I'm not sure if Larson's medicine is that strong."

The old man moved across the room to a broken-down chest, opened the top drawer and pulled out a necklace. He returned to where Jake was standing and held out the necklace.

"Jake," he said, "my grandfather, who was a medicine man, gave me this many years ago. He said it would ward off spirits. And I want you to have it."

Jake took the necklace, which was made up of a section of what looked like eagle claws and a lock of hair. It was strung together with a leather strap and some beads that were placed between each eagle claw. Two feathers hung at what looked like the middle of the necklace.

Jake took the necklace from the old man and stood studying the necklace under the lamp.

"Jake," the old man said, "you need to wear this at all times, especially when you are in your cabin."

Jake slipped the necklace over his head and stood staring at himself in a small mirror that hung just above the chest.

Jake and the old man talked a while more before Jake said goodbye and thanked the old man for his help. As Jake slipped behind the wheel of the old Jeep, he slipped the necklace off and laid it on the seat.

Jake studied his reflection in the rearview mirror and said out loud, "Damn! I can't believe I've resorted to this," and eyed the necklace on the seat beside him. *What if the old man was right*, he thought to himself, *and the only way to rid myself of this is to burn my cabin down. I can just imagine what Alona would say to all this. She would just love for my cabin to be gone and for me to move back there with her.*

Jake felt his temper rising as he sped the old Jeep back down Teesateskie Road.

Jake swore again. "Hell no!" he said out loud. "I will find some way to rid my place from all this crap."

At the stop sign at the end of Teesateskie Road, Jake slipped the necklace back over his head and turned the old Jeep in the direction of Upper Creek Road.

Chapter 11

As Jake pulled up in the yard, everything looked normal. He could see Dexter sleeping on the back porch, and his horse waiting by the barn. *Still no chickens,* he thought as he climbed out of the Jeep. Jake walked over to the hog pen and saw that both hogs were still there. *Maybe the hogs are too heavy for what took my chickens,* he thought.

Jake fed the hogs and put some feed and hay out for his horse before going in the cabin. Everything looked the same as when he had left earlier. Jake sat down in his recliner and Wilson jumped up on his lap and proceeded to go to sleep. Jake was tired and before long he was asleep, also.

Jake wasn't sure how long he had been asleep before a loud noise awakened him. It had gotten dark while he was asleep and he wasn't sure where the sound had come from. He sprang from the recliner and opened the back door. Another sound, and he could tell it was coming from the barn. Jake grabbed the shotgun from over the fireplace and flicked the light on in the barn. He ran across the yard and up to the barn. From where he stood, he could see his horse, and something was spooking him. The horse was kicking the inside of the stable.

Jake couldn't see anything that would spook the horse, and upon entering the barn Jake saw what appeared to be a light in the stall. As he neared the stall, the horse started kicking the wall between the stable where Jake kept the horse feed. The light seemed to be all over the stall and didn't seem to have an origin.

As Jake reached for the stall door, a blast of cold hair hit him full in the face, almost sending him backwards. As Jake fought to maintain his balance, he noticed that the light had gone out in the stall and he was left standing with just the one light in the barn. The horse was still spooked and Jake was worried that he would bust through the door of the stall.

"Whoa, boy!" Jake almost shouted as he calmed the horse. After a few moments the horse started to calm down. Jake opened the stall and went to the horse. The horse was almost lathered up. Putting his hand on the horse, he could feel him shaking all over.

"Easy, boy," Jake said in a soothing tone.

After a few minutes of talking and petting the horse, he finally stopped shaking. Jake stayed for some time in the stall with the horse, and after checking for any way to explain the light he had seen, he headed back to the house. He knew in the back of his mind that there was no way to explain the light in the barn, the same way he could never explain the light at the baptizin' hole.

As Jake neared the back porch, a sound caught his ear. With Jake's hearing problems, he couldn't tell where it came from. He stood on the back porch and listened intently. Then there it was, the same sound he had heard on the trail except now it sounded more like a cry. Then he heard it again, the sound of a child crying. Jake felt the hair stand up on his neck and a chill ran up his back, but for some reason he didn't feel as scared as he had that day when he first heard the sound.

He walked to the edge of the porch and stood trying to hear the sound again. The only sound he could hear was Dexter snoring.

"Durn dog," Jake said out loud, "you didn't even wake up to all the noise in the barn," or what he had just heard.

The rest of Jake's night went without incident and he slept until 8:30 in the morning before crawling out of bed. After making a pot of coffee, he sat in the recliner and thought about all Will Hardy had said. Nothing seemed to make any sense anymore, the missing chickens and the horse almost kicking the barn down and what Jake had heard last night.

After cooking breakfast, Jake decided it was time for him to go get Larson Bearmeat. He knew that it would be a while before Larson would help him kill the hogs and the two boys would want to come and help. But now he was going to go get Larson, and he hoped that he could put an end to everything that had been happening.

The old Jeep bounced along the road that led up Slay Bacon Mountain to where Larson Bearmeat lived. It was just after 10 a.m. when Jake pulled the old Jeep into Larson's front yard. A flock of chickens flew when Jake stepped out of the Jeep and made his way to Larson's front door. Two hound dogs asleep on the porch acknowledged Jake by looking up and wagging their tails. An old couch at the end of the porch was home to two black cats and two hound puppies. The porch reminded Jake of the old house that he had grown up in, where after supper his dad would relax with a cup of coffee and smoke.

As Jake's thoughts went back there, sadness engulfed him for a moment as he realized that after all these years he still missed his dad.

Jake could remember his dad telling stories, as he sat in his rocking chair, about how his life had been as a child. One particular story was about him and his brother walking to school on the railroad tracks in the winter and his brother Baxter betting him a penny he would stick his tongue to the railroad track. Jake's dad had taken the bet, and when he stuck his tongue to the track it had stuck and part of his tongue came off when he pulled free from the track.

Jake stood thinking for a few moments before knocking on Larson's front door.

"Come in, Jake," he heard Larson say.

Jake pushed the door open and stepped inside Larson's living room. It reminded Jake of old man Will Hardy's living room. Larson was seated on a couch and an Indian blanket was draped over the back. A wood stove sat in the corner of the room and it felt like it was at least 90 degrees in the room. Old pictures hung on the wall, and Jake recognized one as being Alona's mother, Annie Bearmeat. An antique shotgun was propped up against the front door.

"Been hunting?" Jake inquired.

"No."

"The darn coyotes have been killing my chickens," Larson replied. "I managed to kill two of them yesterday, but not before I lost three chickens. You want a cup of coffee?"

"Sure," Jake replied.

Larson went into the kitchen and produced two cups of coffee. Jake sat down on the couch and took a swallow of coffee.

"Larson," Jake said, "I was hoping you could go over today with your medicine bag and see what you could do."

Jake told Larson about what had happened with the horse almost kicking the barn down and the voice he had heard.

Larson thought a moment before speaking. "You know, there is a possibility that my medicine may not be strong enough. I want you to keep that in mind."

"Yes, I know," Jake replied, remembering what Will Hardy had said.

Larson got up and moved to the stove where he put another stick of wood in the already hot fire.

"Well, let me round up a few things," Larson said, "and we can get going."

He moved around the living room to a door that Jake figured was his bedroom. After a few minutes he emerged holding a leather pouch and a turtle shell rattle. Jake knew that the turtle shell mounted on a small hickory stick and filled with small stones was used in ceremonies and by medicine men.

Larson moved to an old dresser next to the front door, and after looking through three or four drawers came up with another small leather pouch that he put in his jacket pocket.

"Okay, I'm ready, White Boy," as he flashed a smiled toward Jake.

When Jake turned off Rocky Creek Road and started up his driveway, Larson held up his hand and said, "Stop the Jeep, Jake!"

Jake slid to a stop next to the remains of an old house. Larson got out of the Jeep and walked toward the old house.

"What is it?" Jake asked.

Larson didn't say anything. He just stared toward the mountain where Jake's cabin was. Jake got out of the Jeep and moved in beside the old man. There was a look of concern on Larson's face and for a minute he thought he could see fear in the old man's eyes.

Larson said quietly, "Jake, I can feel the spirits and they know I'm coming. They are strong spirits and they are not going to leave this place without a fight."

Jake went back to the Jeep and got the necklace from the glove box that Will Hardy had given to him. He held it out to the old man and said, "Larson, would it help if I wore this when we go up there?"

The old man held the necklace for a moment before handing it back to Jake.

"Jake," he said, "it sure wouldn't hurt none."

Jake slipped the necklace over his head and immediately felt a strange power like nothing he had ever felt before. It was as if he had been given a second sight.

A fog arose surrounding Jake and from the midst of the fog he could hear chanting. It was as if he could hear the chanting coming from every direction. Fear gripped him like a vise and every muscle in his body seemed paralyzed. Jake didn't know how long all this went on, but after what seemed like an eternity the fog lifted and he was again standing by Larson.

Larson spoke, "Jake, your necklace is powerful medicine and what you felt is just the beginning."

Jake felt like pulling the necklace off, but decided against it. If this was what Jake was in for, then he better get prepared for the worst.

Jake and Larson climbed back in the Jeep and headed up the mountain. After going a short distance, the old Jeep started sputtering and finally came to a halt just below Jake's cabin.

"Jake," Larson said, "I believe that we are going to have to walk the rest of the way."

Larson collected his two leather bags and his turtle rattler and a feather he had picked up as they had left the house. Both men started walking up the road. As they neared the cabin, Jake knew for sure that everything wasn't going to be easy. A fog hung over the cabin just like the one from a few weeks ago.

Dexter was in the road as Jake and Larson neared the cabin. The old dog was trembling. Jake immediately thought of Wilson and, for a moment, wished that he had taken him when he went to get Larson. Jake dropped to his knee and started petting the old dog. If an animal can show fear, Jake sure saw it that day in the eyes of that old dog.

Chapter 12

The fog surrounding the cabin was thick and the cabin was barely visible. Jake glanced toward the barn, and from where he stood he couldn't see the horse. A closer look toward the hog pen confirmed his fear. The two hogs were nowhere in sight.

Larson took the toe of his shoe and scratched a line from one side of the road to the other. From one of his leather pouches he pulled a small jar. He opened the jar and with his thumb and forefinger pinched a small amount of white powder. He sprinkled the powder in the lines that he had drawn from one side of the road to the other.

"Jake, he said, "I want you to stay on the other side of the line. This will keep the spirits away from you."

Larson," Jake replied, "I'm really worried about Wilson and I feel like I ought to go check on him."

"No, Jake," Larson stated, "I will go get him for you."

Jake watched the old man as he walked up the road and went to the back door. Jake could feel the presence of something and he stepped back until he was behind the line in the road. Jake touched the necklace around his neck and for a moment felt like he was going to be swept away. He staggered and almost fell. It was as if some unseen force was trying to choke the life out of him and he was finding it hard to breathe.

Jake could see Larson on the back porch and it seemed like everything was floating around him. He tried to yell out, but no sound came. He felt himself falling and the darkness rushing in. He grasped the necklace even tighter and for a moment everything stopped moving and he was able to keep himself from falling.

Larson had gone in the cabin and emerged holding Wilson in his arms. The little dog didn't seem to be moving. Jake wanted to run to Larson and get Wilson, but he was only able to yell out in a small voice. Jake was on his knees, and when he tried to stand the whole world started to spin.

Larson made his way to where Jake was and handed him Wilson. There was sweat on the old man's brow, and Jake could see that he was having a hard time breathing. Jake took Wilson in his arms and sat down on the ground. The little dog was breathing, and Jake could detect a slow heartbeat.

"What happened to him?" Jake almost shouted at Larson.

"Well, Jake," he replied, "the spirits have taken a lot out of him. They feed on anything that is alive."

Jake kept petting Wilson, and the little dog finally opened his eyes and tried to lick Jake's hand. Jake could feel the tears coming and found himself praying for a miracle to save his best friend.

Chapter 13

Larson took a small cup from one of the leather bags. It had been fashioned out of a gourd with the stem of the gourd acting as the handle. Larson pulled what Jake thought was the tassel from an ear of corn from the other leather bag. He crumpled up the grass-like substance and placed it in the cup.

The fog still hung heavy over the cabin as Larson made his way to the corner of the cabin. From within the fog Jake could hear the chanting again. What looked like dark shadows were coming out of the fog and were surrounding Larson. The shadows seemed to Jake like they were trying to attack Larson. The fear in Jake rose and he was afraid for the old man.

Larson got to the corner of the cabin, and after a minute set fire to the contents of the cup. From his shirt pocket he pulled the feather and, as he waved it over the burning cup, Jake could hear screams coming from within the fog and the chanting getting louder to the point that he was tempted to cover his ears.

Larson kept waving the feather over the pot, which now had burned out and only a thin stream of smoke rose from the cup. Jake was finding it hard to believe what was going on in front of him. The shadows were getting faster and they seemed to land where Larson was on his knees at the corner of the cabin.

The day was getting darker and Jake noticed that a large group of clouds had gathered over the mountain. From the clouds, Jake could hear the thunder, and the lightning was starting to hit around the cabin. The air seemed to be filled with something sinister and the rain was starting to fall. The thunder was so loud that Jake thought it was going to split the earth open. In the rain, Jake was having a hard time seeing Larson, who was still on his knees continuing to wave the feather over the cup. Everything in Jake told him to go help the old man, but when he tried to move it was like he was pinned to the ground.

By this time the rain was coming in torrents and Jake felt himself slowly drifting into a black hole and felt himself falling as the darkness invaded him.

Chapter 14

From somewhere in the darkness, Jake could hear laughter, children laughing. As the darkness was swept away, Jake found himself standing in a valley. Small log huts adorned the hillside and a number of Indian children were playing with a homemade ball. They all stopped when they saw Jake and the tallest boy, who Jake took to be about 12 or 13 years old, walked toward Jake while the others stood at a distance. When they started talking, Jake recognized the language as Cherokee.

The tall boy stopped a shout's distance from Jake and stood staring at him before speaking. Jake's knowledge of the Cherokee language was limited, and when the boy spoke Jake recognized the word for hello "she-o." Jake replied, and the boy smiled for a moment. The next words out of the boy's mouth were beyond Jake's comprehension. The other children had moved up behind the tall boy and continued to speak among themselves.

Jake observed the valley that he was in and something about it was familiar. Jake counted 10 huts which were made from logs with mud in between the logs and chimneys that were made from rock. There was smoke coming from three of them. A small stream ran just below the last hut.

Jake recognized a corn pounder, which was a section of log that had been hollowed out and a long pole was used to smash the kernels into cornmeal. Just up the valley Jake could see a cornfield, and judging from the corn he could tell that it was autumn. There were animal hides hanging from a pole that had been lodged on top of two poles that had been put in the ground. Jake could tell that one of the hides was from a bear and two more looked like they were from raccoons.

A small igloo-shaped structure stood next to the stream. It was covered with hides. Jake figured that it must be a sweat lodge, a place where stones were heated and water was poured over them to make steam. This was done for cleansing of the spirit or for ceremonies that were held in the village.

A section of log about 12 feet long was particularly hewn out, and Jake knew that it was a canoe in the making. He stood staring at the boy, who now had moved away and back to the group of other children. There were nine children ranging from what Jake figured was 5 years to 12 or 14 years old. Jake couldn't figure why he was here or what year he was in. From everything around him, he figured it was in the 1800s. But how did he get there and how was he going to get back to his cabin and Larson?

From one of the huts, Jake saw the door open and a tall Indian lady emerge. She looked to be in her 40s or early 50s. She was dressed in a long dress that had been fashioned from an animal hide. Her black hair hung down to her waist and a beaded headband adorned her head. On her feet were a beautiful pair of moccasins. Her beauty was astounding even at her age.

She stood looking at Jake for some time, and when she moved she stepped in front of Jake. When she smiled, her teeth were flawless. The smile made her even more beautiful. Jake felt like he was in a dream, and when he tried to speak he found nothing would come out.

"Jake, my son," she spoke, "it is good that you are here."

She reached out and took Jake's head between her hands. Her voice sounded far away, and he was surprised that he could understand her.

Finally Jake spoke. "Where am I?" he asked.

"You are back here with your people," she answered.

"How did I get here?" Jake asked.

"You were brought here for a purpose, my son."

"Why do you keep saying 'my son'?" he asked.

"Jake," she said slowly," you were sent here to help someone find something."

"How do you know my name?" he asked. "And what is your name?"

"My name is Tu-Tehia, which means Snow Bird, and, Jake, you are my great-great-great-grandson."

Jake was speechless. After a few moments, he asked, "How can I be your grandson?"

"My child," she spoke, "you are in the spirit world where anything is possible. I have been with you all these years and I will be with you until it is time for you to join us here. Come with me and I will show you what you need to do."

As they moved through the village, the children moved aside and went back to playing with their ball. Like in a dream, Jake felt himself and the woman move to the top of the mountain that overlooked the village. From the top of the mountain Jake could see for miles. The autumn colors were breathtaking.

Tu-Tehia stood beside Jake and pointed to the mountaintop. Then Jake recognized where he was at. The mountaintop that she was pointing at was where Jake had built his cabin.

"Jake," she spoke, "there is a battle going on up there between good and evil. The spirits that Larson is fighting with are strong, and I only hope that he can defeat them. The spirits were left here to protect the sacred burial ground, and to drive them away would take a miracle. But, my son, that is not what you are here for. Soon I will leave the village and go into the mountains where I shall die. My time has come and I can feel the spirit world calling for me to go. The only way you can see me now is that you have traveled here in your mind. You must go back and help Larson."

"But it is so peaceful here," Jake protested, "and I wish that I could stay here and live in this time with you."

"Like I said, Jake, there will be a time when we can be together, but now you must go."

"Well, what is it you want me to do?" he asked.

When Tu-Tehia spoke, Jake could hear a sadness in her voice.

"Jake," she said, "when I leave the village, my granddaughter, whose name is Tu-Tehia also, will follow and she will be lost in the mountains and will never return to the village. I know you have heard the legend about the small girl that searches for her grandmother. Well, that legend is true. And, Jake, I know that you have heard her around your cabin. And she will haunt you until you help her find the way to where my bones are hidden in the mountains. I can't tell you exactly where they are; you will have to find that out for yourself."

Tu-Tehia turned to Jake and indicated a place in the woods and said, "Jake, you sit there, for the time is short."

Both Jake and Tu-Tehia sat down. She put her arm around Jake. As if a blanket of darkness had settled over them, Jake felt himself slipping away as the sound of her voice slowly took Jake into the darkness.

Chapter 15

"Jake, wake up!"

The voice sounded far away and he struggled to pull himself out of the darkness.

"Jake, wake up!" the voice said again.

He could feel the wet earth pressing against his cheek. Jake slowly opened his eyes and tried to pull himself up from the ground. He felt Wilson beside him and immediately thought of Larson bringing the dog to him.

"Easy does it, Jake."

He recognized Larson's voice.

"It's all over, Jake," he heard the old man say.

Jake picked up Wilson and the dog immediately started licking him in the face.

"What happened?" Jake asked.

"You passed out," the old man replied.

Jake started telling Larson about the dream that he had and how he had met his great-great-great-grandmother. The old man listened intently and a smile came over his face.

"Well, Jake," he replied, "you went to a place that I have seen in a vision and it's a place where things are different. There is no death, no pain, only happiness. Someday soon I hope to go there."

Jake finished telling Larson all that he had seen and heard and how Tu-Tehia had told him that he needed to help her granddaughter find the place where she had died.

The old man thought for a moment before speaking. "Well, Jake, that is something that you will have to figure out on your own. There is one thing I can tell you. The legend goes that the grandmother went to a place that the Indians call 'Om-ga-doe-we-shu'. That means falling water. It is a place filled with waterfalls and the terrain is very rough. I think it is located at the start of Webb Creek. I have been there on a couple of occasions and it is a beautiful place."

Jake stood for a few moments before speaking. "Well, Larson," he said, "do you think that your medicine worked on getting rid of the spirits around this place?"

"Well," Larson replied, "Jake, did you notice that your horse is back, along with the hogs and your chickens?"

"Jake," Larson said, "I believe that they were here all along, it's just that you couldn't see them. The spirits have a way of blinding you to certain things."

"Well," Jake replied, "I hope everything here is back to normal and I can get back to my life."

"Jake," Larson replied, "I hope that things will get back to normal, but I'm not sure if we have gotten rid of them for good. They are strong, and don't be surprised if they do come back."

Jake picked Wilson up and held him for a long time before putting him down. The little dog immediately ran off to where a cluster of chickens stood and chased them back toward the henhouse.

"Well," Larson spoke, "since the hogs are back, I guess we could figure on killing them pretty soon. I'm sure the boys will be happy to hear that."

"One more thing," Jake said. "How do you get the spirit of the little girl to go with me to Webb Creek, and how do I start looking for someone who has been dead for 150 years or more?"

"Well, Jake," Larson said, "I will have to go with you and we will have to perform a ritual once we find out where the old lady died, and that way maybe we can summon her spirit to where we are."

Chapter 16

The trip back up to Slay Bacon Mountain to drop off Larson was pretty much uneventful. Larson talked about the days when he was a child and how he had killed his first bear on Slay Bacon Mountain. Jake told Larson about him seeing the deer when he had come to see Larson and how it had almost spooked his horse. Jake and Larson talked about getting together and going hunting in the future.

After Jake had dropped Larson off, he took his time making the trip back to his cabin. As he neared Rocky Creek, he stopped and got his fishing pole out and chose a Booster tailspinner. Jake's favorite fishing hole was just a ways up Rocky Creek, and as he made his way up the creek he thought of his dad and how they had fished the stream together and how his dad would let him pull the fish in after he had hooked them.

Jake arrived at his fishing hole. After the rain, the creek was up and the waterfall sent a spray of water that when it hit the sun created a beautiful rainbow. Jake fished for a few moments before he felt something hit his line. As he jerked the line and attempted to reel it in, the line only got tighter. Whatever had ahold of the line was stronger than any fish that Jake had ever pulled out of Rocky Creek. Jake continued to pull on the line, which had gotten to the point that he thought it was going to break his pole. The line started to make a circular motion in the creek as if something was going round and round in the water. Jake continued to fight the line, and suddenly his pole gave way and broke. The line snapped hard against Jake and for a moment he thought the entire pole was going to be ripped from his hand.

The water started churning and a giant whirlpool was starting to form. Jake stepped back away from the creek, afraid that he might be pulled into it. He stood watching the whirlpool and from the creek rose a mist and a figure starting to form just above the water.

"Oh, shit," Jake said out loud, "not again."

The figure hung over the water, and as it formed more Jake could make out what looked like a small child with its arms outstretched toward him. The child was a small girl, and he could tell that it was an Indian girl. She wore a dress like Jake had seen in the Indian village, and a pair of moccasins adorned her feet. Her hair hung down to her waist the way Tu-Tehia's had, and she wore a headband in the same fashion as Tu-Tehia's.

The little girl held her hands out toward Jake and for a moment he thought that she was going to touch him. When she spoke, it was in the Cherokee language. Jake recognized the word "E-li-she" as being grandmother. The other words she spoke led Jake to think that she meant—help me find my grandmother.

A cry emerged from the figure as she slowly vanished into the mist that hung over the creek. As quickly as she had vanished, the creek returned to its normal state and Jake was left standing on the creek bank.

Jake made his way back down Rocky Creek. And after putting what was left of his fishing pole in the Jeep, he sat in the driver's seat for some time thinking about what had taken place, knowing that in the very near future he was going to have to make a trip up Webb Creek and attempt to find where the old lady had died and if, indeed, Webb Creek was the place that she had died.

Chapter 17

For the next week, Jake worked around his cabin and hadn't seen anything out of the way. He was glad that everything seemed to be back to normal, and with each passing day he praised Larson for what he had done. Jake had made up his mind to kill the hogs the coming weekend.

The air was chilly and the leaves were starting to fall. Jake dreaded to call Alona and hear how dangerous it would be for him to have to shoot something and she was afraid that one of the boys would get shot, but he dialed her number anyway, because she would always meet him in town with the boys.

After three rings, she answered and Jake knew that the anger in her voice meant that she was going to give him a hard time.

"Hello," Jake said.

And before he could say anything else, she started. "Well, Jake, I guess it's time to kill those stupid hogs. And you know how I feel about that." She went on to say, "I guess you want me to bring the boys to town?"

Well," Jake replied, "I was hoping that you could. You know that I don't like to come to Snowridge."

"Oh, hell, Jake, you lived out here for 25 years and at least you could make the trip for my sake, if you still love me."

Well," Jake said reluctantly, "okay, I will come out there to pick them up, but I'm not going to stay."

"Well, hell, Jake," she said, "if you don't love me anymore, then give me a divorce so I can get on with my life."

Jake was stunned to hear Alona talk that way and a moment of shock ran through him. He was unsure of what to say next. The line went quiet for a few moments before she finally spoke.

"Jake," she said, "I'm sorry to talk to you that way, but sometimes I feel like you aren't never coming back to me. You know I still love you and I just want you to be happy, even if it does mean staying on that mountain."

"Well, Alona," Jake said, "I still love you. And I hope someday to be back there with you, but not now. Please try to understand that there are a lot of things that I have to deal with and some things I have already done."

Jake told Alona what had happened at the baptizin' hole and how he knew who did those awful things to him. He told her of the face in the laurel and that he knew it was his mother.

"Oh, goodness," Alona replied, "I bet that was a scary thing you had to go through."

"Well," Jake said, "at least that mystery is solved and it feels like something has been lifted from my shoulders. And also, Larson came over and used his medicine, and I think that the spirits are finally gone."

Jake told Alona about the small girl and how he felt it was up to him to try and find the bones of her grandmother.

"Wow," Alona said, "that has been a lot of things that you have been through. I bet it has taken a lot out of you and I hope you are getting a lot of rest."

"Well, Jake said, "I feel a lot better and I'm getting a lot of rest. Me and Wilson are sleeping till ten in the morning. Also, I have done a lot of work around the cabin and barn. When we kill the hogs, I will bring you some of the meat and pork chops and sausage, and I know that you will want the head so you can have the brains and eyes."

Alona's voice had settled down, and after chatting for some time he promised to come to Snowridge and pick up the boys.

The week went by fast and before Jake even realized it, it was Friday. Jake headed out towards Snowridge, and before he knew it he was sitting in front of the house that he had built. Jake loved the way that Alona kept the place beautiful with all the flowers that were now starting to shed their leaves.

Victor and Jasper keep the yard mowed and help Alona with all the yard work. And she still managed to raise a small garden, and Jake could see what was called "Leather Britches" hanging on the porch. Leather Britches are green beans that have been sewn with the needle going through the middle and then would be hung out to dry. Jake loved Leather Britches and he hoped Alona would give him some of them.

The front door opened and both Victor and Jasper came through as if to see how quickly they could get to where Jake was sitting. Both boys tried to talk at the same time and, after hugging Jake, started with the questions.

"Well, Papaw," Victor said, "are we going to kill the hogs tomorrow?"

"Well, boys," Jake replied, "I was planning to kill them tomorrow. I will have to go and get Larson tomorrow, and then we will kill them."

Jake noticed that Alona had come out on the front porch and was watching them intently. He got out of the Jeep and walked to where Alona was standing. She was a beautiful woman and had always kept herself as someone who was a pleasure to look at. She walked down the steps and came to Jake. He put his arms around her and she put hers around him. They embraced for a short while and then Jake kissed her. She returned the kiss and said, "Well, it's good to see you, stranger."

"Well," Jake responded, "it's good to see you, too. It has been awhile."

Both Jasper and Victor had joined Jake and Alona and were arguing about who got to ride in the front seat going back to Rocky Creek.

"Boys," Alona interrupted, "why don't you two get your clothes while I talk to your papa?"

Both boys made a beeline back through the front door. Victor came back on the porch and said, "Papaw, can I take my rifle to shoot the hogs with?"

"Sure thing, son," Jake replied.

Alona gave Jake a stern look and said, "Are you sure the boys will be okay and not get shot?"

"Sure they will be okay," Jake said. "I'm going to let Jasper kill one of the hogs and Victor kill the other one ... and Larson will be there helping us, too."

"Jake," Alona said, "are you sure that Larson got rid of the spirits?"

"Well," Jake said, "nothing has happened in the past three weeks, and I'm pretty sure that they are gone."

"Well, Jake," Alona said, "will you promise to bring them back if anything does happen, no matter what time?"

"Now, Alona," Jake said, "there is nothing that is going to happen up there and the boys should have a good time."

"Well, Jake," Alona said, "do you remember us talking about going to see a marriage counselor?"

"Oh, yea," Jake said. "I will go with you as soon as I get a few things done around the cabin."

"You know something, Jake? You are always coming up with an excuse every time I try and talk with you about going."

"Well, Alona, I don't mean to put you off, but there are things that I need to do like kill the hogs and the work that goes into preparing the meat and putting it up for the winter. I have decided this year I am going to can some of the meat, and I will give you whatever you need this winter."

"Jake," Alona said, "all that means nothing to me. I just want to be with you."

"Alona," Jake said, "I hope that someday we can be together, but there are still things that I need to work on. One thing I feel better about is the experience I went through at the swimming hole. Now I don't have to keep on reliving what happened a long time ago. I know now who they were and I'm trying to forgive them. That part has been hard to do. But I'm slowly getting there, and hopefully someday I can totally forgive them."

"I know, Jake," Alona said, "that would mean a lot to you. And maybe someday you can put all those things behind you."

"Well," Jake asked, "where are the girls? I was hoping to see them."

"Well, Jake, they are with their mother, and every time they go with her they come back crying and I can't do anything."

"Well, I'm sorry to hear that," Jake said. "You know that she has a right to be with them. I only wish we could take her back to court and get full custody of the girls."

"Well, I wish that would happen," Alona said, "but I don't want to drag the girls through that again. They had a hard time when we went through the whole mess before."

The boys had come back out and Victor was carrying his .22 rifle by his side. Jake saw a frown on Alona's face when she saw the rifle.

She turned to Jake with a frown and said, "You had better keep an eye on both of them."

Jake smiled at Alona and said, "Don't worry. I won't let them have the rifle unless I am with them, and I might even let them target practice at a tin can."

Jake turned to Victor and said, "Did you hear what I just told your grandma? By the way, do you have shells for the .22?"

Victor produced five .22 shells.

"Well," Jake said, "We will have to stop at A-4 Home Center and get a box."

Jake had done a lot of talking to Victor about the danger of a gun and how to use it, and Victor seemed to pay close attention to what Jake had said. It was Jasper that he was worried about. Jasper hadn't shown any interest in learning about how dangerous they could be and he was always saying, "Just shoot them," when the conversation turned to someone that they didn't like.

After a few minutes of Alona telling them to be good and to mind Jake when he told them to do something, they were headed back to Rocky Branch. For some reason, Jake wanted to stop at Dent's Cafe. Both boys had told Jake that they were hungry. So after a short stop at A-4 for the shells, they headed to Dent's Cafe.

When they entered the cafe, Jake saw Willow Reid taking an order from a couple of teenagers and one of them seemed to be pestering Willow and was trying to put his hands on her. Jake thought that Willow was going to smack him dead in the face. Jake smiled, and after seating the boys he walked over to where the two teenagers were sitting. Willow looked at Jake and smiled. Jake faced the two boys and said, "Don't you boys know it's not nice to put your grubby little paws on the lady here?"

Both of the boys looked at each other and said, "Well, looks like the old man here don't like our company and would like us to leave."

"Well," the other one said jokingly, "reckon he is man enough to make us leave?"

Before the other one could say anything, Jake had both of them by the nose, leading them to the door. Bill Lewis was watching Jake with a smile.

After Jake had deposited the two young boys in the parking lot and come back in the restaurant, Bill came over to him and said, "Well, Jake, I'm glad you done that. I have trouble out of those two all the time."

Bill Lewis had been running Dent's Cafe as long as Jake could remember.

Willow walked up and smiled. "Wow, my knight in shining armor."

Jake smiled and said, "Well, I'm glad I could bluff them out of here."

Jake made his way back to where the boys were. They both were smiling, and Jasper said, "Wow, Papaw, you sure showed them the door."

Jake replied, "It was nothing, boys. Now, let's see, what do you two want to eat?"

Willow had come over to the table and proceeded to take their orders. The boys ordered hamburgers and fries and Jake took the special, a hamburger steak with baked potato and slaw.

Jake sat thinking about why he had stopped at the restaurant and finally came to the conclusion that he had wanted to see Willow and he didn't really care who saw him.

Willow came back to the table and refilled his cup with coffee. She was standing next to Jake, and he felt a tingle run up his spine.

Damn, he thought, *why do I feel this way? I might as well admit it ... I want her.*

Jake thought of Alona and cursed himself for being so weak. As Willow poured his coffee, she let her left hand brush up against Jake's. That sent a tingle up his arm. Willow smiled at Jake and then went on to another table.

Jake found it hard to think straight, and after a few minutes he made his way to the counter to pay his and the boys' tab. Willow took his money and touched his hand again as she gave him back his change.

Wow, Jake thought, *I haven't felt this way for a long time.*

There was no question as to the fact that he wanted Willow Reid.

Outside the cafe, Victor asked, "Papaw, can I drive? I have my permit, and Mamaw lets me drive her around."

"Well," Jake said, "Victor, do you know how to drive a stick? It's different than driving an automatic."

"Well, Papaw," Victor said, "I have drove my friend's pickup and it's a stick."

"Well," Jake said, "I guess you could try it, but you have to drive slowly and watch where you are going."

"Okay, Papaw, I will be careful and I will take my time."

Jake felt strange sitting in the passenger side of the old Jeep as they headed up Rocky Branch. He was impressed at how well Victor handled the old Jeep and how he drove carefully along the old road that led up to the cabin. When they arrived at the cabin, Victor parked the old Jeep next to the back porch.

"Okay, boys," Jake said, "we have to get something done so we can get ready to kill the hogs. First thing we have to do is build a tripod to hang the hogs on, and then we have to set up the old washtub to boil the water to help get the hair off. Boys, I hope you two are rested up, because tomorrow is going to be a long day."

Jake spoke to the boys and asked them if they wanted to go see Larson. Jake figured he had better go see Larson and make sure the old man felt like helping butcher the hogs. The boys informed Jake that they would love to go and see their great-great uncle.

Jake let Victor drive them up to Larson's house. When they arrived, they found Larson sitting on the front porch holding a shotgun.

"What's going on?" Jake inquired.

"It's them coyotes again. They managed to get two more of my chickens, and I didn't even get a shot at them?"

"Well, Jake," Larson said, "where did you get them fine looking boys you got there?"

The boys jumped from the Jeep and hurried up to the porch. Then both of them tried to hug Larson at the same time.

"Well," Larson said, "you boys have grown a lot since the last time I got to see you two. Are you minding your grandma and helping her around the house?"

Both boys answered that they were doing everything Alona asked them to do.

"Well," Larson said, "I was thinking about my old Jeep. And I'm not ever going to fix it back up, and I was wondering if you, Victor, would be interested in taking it and fixing it up. I don't think that there is a lot to do to the old thing. And then, when you get your license, you will have something to drive to school in ... or maybe you might be too ashamed of it to be caught dead in the old thing?"

"Oh, no, I would love to drive it to school," Victor said enthusiastically.

"I've always thought that with a little work and new wheels it would be the perfect rig to fix up. And I bet that Jake would love to help you fix it up."

"Well," Victor said, "I bet Papaw would love to help us work on the Jeep. You know he restored the Jeep he drives, and it sure does run good."

Jake spoke up and said, "Boys, what have you gotten me into this time? I got to take a piss, and when I get back you two boys have got me a job," he said with a smile. "Sure thing. I would love to help with the old Jeep, and maybe you two might learn something in the process."

Five o'clock in the morning came early and Jake was having a hard time getting the boys up. Larson had cooked up a big breakfast.

"Wow!" Jasper said. "What time is it, anyway? It's still dark outside."

"Well," Larson responded, "it's five o'clock in the morning ... time for all to get up and face the day."

"Well, Jasper," Jake said, "would you go and let the horse out into the pasture and feed him some oats? The flashlight is on the table, and I will turn on the light in the barn to help you see when you let the horse out. You come back so we can eat the good breakfast that Larson has cooked. I'm sure that you boys will like it. There is eggs and sausage with a pan of gravy and biscuits, and we will have some homemade jelly and honey."

By this time, Jasper had gotten up and was staring at the food that Larson had cooked. Larson had chosen to spend the night so Jake wouldn't have to get up early. Few words were spoken at the breakfast table, and before long Jake could see the sun starting to come up. After washing the breakfast dishes and putting them away, it was time to start getting the fire built to boil the water.

Jake told Victor to go in the cabin and get his rifle. By the time Victor brought the gun out, Larson had already started a fire under the old wash pot.

"Okay, boys, who wants to go first and send one of them hogs to 'the promised land'?"

Victor moved over to the hog pen and looked at Jasper. "Do you want to shoot the first one?" he asked.

"Well, I was hoping that you would let me go first."

"Okay," Victor said. "Here is my rifle."

Jake spoke up and said, "You both should know how dangerous it is and how it only takes once to get yourself hurt or killed. And, Jasper, you haven't been around guns enough to know how to handle a gun, so this is where you start learning."

Jake got a couple of cans and set them on the bank about 20 feet away. He gave Jasper two shells, and after showing him where to load the rifle and how to aim he told him to go ahead and shoot. Jake thought of what Alona had said and how she was worried one of the boys would get hurt, or worse. The shot made Jake jump as he realized he had been daydreaming. He moved to where the cans were at and noticed that there was a small hole in the side of one of them.

"Wow," Jake said," that's good shooting."

Jasper had come up to where Jake was standing.

"Wow," he said, "I hit it, didn't I?"

"Yes, you sure did, Jasper. Now I want you to shoot the hog right between the eyes. Just take your time and everything will be okay."

Jake had noticed that Jasper was trembling and he was worried that he might miss and shoot someone. Jake spoke up and asked Jasper, "Why are you shaking?"

Jasper responded, "I'm so excited that I can't seem to stop. But I will be okay."

"Are you sure you're okay?" asked Jake.

"Yes, I will be okay."

"Okay," Jake said. "Let's go send Jed to the Promised Land."

"Okay, Papaw," Jasper said, "let's go."

Jasper reloaded the rifle and made his way to the hog pen. After a few minutes, Jasper put the barrel between Jed's eyes and pulled the trigger. The big hog fell down, and after a few moments he was still.

"Wow, Jasper, that was good," said Victor, and they both started laughing.

Jake moved over to where the boys were standing.

"Okay, boys. How did Jasper learn to shoot that good?"

Both boys looked at each other, and after a few moments Victor confessed, "Well, Papaw, you never showed Jasper how to shoot, and he wanted to learn, so when Mamaw would leave the house we would go into the woods and practice shooting. My friend would get us a couple of boxes of shells at A-4 and we kept them hid in the barn. We didn't do that to be mean, but you were always gone, and we were always safe when we went in the woods. And to tell the truth, Jasper can outshoot me any day. Please don't tell Mamaw what we would do when she was gone to work."

Jake didn't say anything for a few minutes, and then finally he spoke. "Boys, I can understand what you were doing, and I'm as much to blame as you are. But you have got to tell your Mamaw when we get back to your house. But we can talk about that later. So right now we have two hogs that need to be butchered."

Jasper gave Victor his rifle back, and then Jake spoke up and said, "Let's fix this one hog before we shoot the other one."

And so the day had officially begun. They had to drag the hog to where Jake and Larson had built the tripod. Jake, the boys and Larson tied the hog's back legs together, and it took all of them to lift the hog in the air. Before long the hog was hanging from its back legs. Larson asked the boys if either one of them wanted to cut the hog's throat. Jasper quickly spoke up and said he wanted to do it. Larson pulled a large hunting knife out and handed it to Jasper.

"Now, remember, cut the throat deep," Larson said, "so all the blood will drain out."

Jasper put the knife against the hog's throat and started to cut. He made the incision from right to left, and when the blood gushed Jasper jumped and dropped the hunting knife. Jake picked the knife up and handed it back to Jasper.

"Jasper, you have to finish up so all the blood will drain."

Jasper stood watching the blood pour out of the hog. Then he handed the knife back to Jake and said, "I don't think I can do it."

For a moment, Jake saw tears well up in Jasper's eyes.

"Okay, son, I won't make you do it."

Larson took the knife from Jake and with one single slice he cut a deep gash from ear to ear on the hog. Jasper walked a short distance away and then sat down on the ground. Jake followed him and knelt down to next to him.

"What happened, son?" he inquired.

"Well, Papaw," Jasper stuttered, "you are not going to believe this.

But when I started to cut the hog's throat and I seen all the blood, the hog spoke to me and his eyes moved. I couldn't understand what it was saying, but it sounded like it said 'leave this place. '"

Jake felt a chill that went all the way up his spine to his head.

Jasper pleaded, "Please don't tell Mamaw. She won't let me or Victor come up here anymore. And please don't tell Larson ... he will laugh at me. And if this gets back to school, all the kids will laugh at me and call me coward."

"Okay, Jasper," Jake said, "it will be between you and me and no one else will ever have to know. Jasper, do you feel like helping us finish the hogs?"

"Well, I will try and help you."

"And if you don't want to, that will be okay."

"Okay, Papaw, let's go and get started."

Through the day they gutted and used the hot water to help loosen the hair. Finally, in the afternoon, they had both of the hogs dressed out. Jake figured there were at least 200 pounds of meat. So after taking Larson home, they set out to the packing house to drop the meat off. Then they all went into Judson to get something to eat at Dent's Cafe. The boys looked like they had been in battle because they had blood on their faces, and after going to the bathroom they still didn't look much better.

Willow Reid took their order, and again the boys ordered hamburgers and fries and Jake ordered the special, chicken livers with greens and potatoes with coleslaw. Both boys had turned their noses up when Jake tried to get them to try the special. Jake had loved chicken livers as long as he could remember. His dad had eaten them, also. Willow brought their food, and after a smile and touching Jake's arm, they all set about eating their food.

Jake couldn't help thinking about what Jasper had said earlier about the hog that had spoken to him. He felt the same as he had before, and now Jake knew that the medicine that Larson had used up on the cabin hadn't completely gotten rid of the spirits around the cabin. Jake also thought about the little girl and how she came to Jake in the whirlpool and how she had broken the fishing pole and was so close to him that day that he could almost touch her.

Jake had been putting off going up Webb Creek because, to tell the truth, he was scared to go up there to try and find the place where Jake's great-great-great-grandmother had died. Jake knew he needed to find the place and help the little girl to move on to where she could be at peace and be with her grandmother and all the ones that had gone before. He almost wished he could be there, too.

The two boys had already finished their meals and had ordered some peach cobbler for dessert. Willow managed to touch Jake's arm while collecting the dishes. If one thing was for sure, she wanted to be with Jake.

After paying their tab, Jake and the boys headed back to the meat processing plant. Jake had gotten pork chops and sausage and the heads of the hogs. The boys always spent two nights, and Jake always looked forward to their visits and a chance to spend more time with them.

"Okay, boys," Jake said, "do you all want to have pork chops for supper and sausage for breakfast?"

They both informed Jake that they would love to eat sausage in the morning and pork chops in the evening at supper.

"Well, boys," Jake spoke, "we had better get a couple of bags of ice to keep Alona's hog's head so they wouldn't spoil."

Jake sent Victor into the convenience store for the ice. After he had gone into the store, Jake turned to Jasper and said, "Jasper, do you want to talk about what happened up at the cabin?"

"Well ..." Jasper said quietly.

Jake could tell by the tone of his voice that it still scared him to talk about what had taken place on the hill.

"Well," Jake said, "we don't have to talk about it if you would rather not want to."

"No, we can talk if you want to," Jasper said.

"Well," Jake said, "I believe what you told me, and I can relate to what happened to you. You know, Jasper, there has been things happening up there for some time now, and I thought that it was over. Did you know that Larson was a medicine man and that he came over to the cabin and performed a ritual to try and get rid of the spirits that were at the cabin? I knew, when I seen your face, that you had come in contact with the spirits. I want you to promise not to talk to your Mamaw or anyone else ... even Victor. You know that she would worry as long as you were up there with me. I know, Jasper, that the spirits are real, after what I have gone through."

Jake proceeded to tell Jasper about all the strange things that had happened. Jasper listened, and Jake could see the fear in his eyes as he told him about the dream where he thought that Wilson was dead and where the chickens had disappeared and the hogs had disappeared.

"You know, son, I think that I built the cabin on a burial ground. And how the legend goes is that the bad spirits are left here to protect the burial grounds, and they are the ones I think that is doing all this to make me move away from where the cabin is. And I don't want to leave from there, and I sure don't want to burn my cabin down, but I'm almost to the point that I don't know what is left to do."

Victor had gotten back with the ice. And after putting the two heads in the ice chest that Jake brought from the cabin they set out for Rocky Branch.

As Victor made his way in the old Jeep, he said, "Papaw, do you believe in ghosts?"

"Well, I don't know if I do or not," answered Jake. "Why do you ask?"

"Well," Victor continued, "when we were killing the hogs and Jasper was starting to cut the throat of the hog, I saw one of the eyes of the hog blink and I heard something like a voice saying 'leave here' or maybe 'leave this place.' I'm not really sure what it said."

Jake and Jasper looked at each other and then back at Victor.

"Well, Victor," Jake said, "I believe what you are saying is true."

Then Jake proceeded to tell Victor some of the things that he had told Jasper. Both boys looked at each other, and Jake could see the fear in both their eyes. Neither boy said anything until they arrived at the cabin.

Jasper finally spoke up and said, "Papaw, do you think that Uncle Larson would come back and try his medicine one more time?"

"I don't know. I was thinking the same thing," Jake said. "We can go see him and see what he has to say. Okay, let's go."

After they removed the hog meat and put it up, they headed out to Larson's home. The old man was sitting on the front porch, and Jake could tell by the expression on the old man's face that something was wrong. Jake parked the old Jeep and stepped out and made his way up the front steps.

"Hey, White Man," Larson said. "I knew that you would be here today."

"How did you know, Larson?" Jake asked.

"Well, I also heard what the two boys heard and the voice telling us to get out of there and I knew that you would be here sooner or later."

"Well, Larson," Jake said, "we don't know what else to do."

"Well, Jake," Larson said, "there is one other thing that I could do, but it involves Jasper being there with me."

"Really?" Jake said. "Why him?"

"Well, it has to do with someone that is Indian to go with me. Victor is white and it can't be him."

"I just don't know what Alona would say if she knew that her grandson was going through a ritual with me. You know how she is when it comes to things like that. And I was thinking of teaching Jasper to be a medicine man. I think she would be okay with that. And also, together, Jasper and me, we would be a lot stronger. And we also need to go as soon as possible, before the spirits get their strength back."

Both boys had been listening to the conversation between Jake and Larson.

Jasper spoke up and said, "I will go, Papaw, if it means saving the cabin ... and I know that I will be getting that place when I get older."

Larson spoke up. "Now, listen carefully to what I am going to tell you. First of all, you can't get scared and you have to do exactly what I tell you to do. The spirits are still weak. When I done my medicine before, I almost got rid of them, but killing something up there gave them back some of their strength, and I believe that both of us can destroy them once and for all. If we are going to do this, I need to talk to Jasper alone."

"Okay. Jasper, how do you feel about going with Larson?" Jake asked.

"Okay, Papaw, I will go with him and I will try and not get scared."

"Okay," Larson said. "I need to teach you something that you will need to know and it is important that you learn what I have to say. Come on, Jasper, come with me for a few minutes."

Larson got a leather bag and handed it to Jasper. From another drawer he pulled a rattler that had been made from a turtle shell. He also handed Jasper a headband and told him to put it on.

"Okay," Larson said. "Will you and Victor go in the house?"

Jake led the way into Larson's house and he and Victor sat down on the couch. Outside, Larson and Jasper went in a small building just below the house. Inside the building there was an old box sitting on an old dresser in the corner of the building. Larson opened one of the doors on the box and pulled a small jar from inside. The contents looked like flour. Larson took a pinch between his fingers and dusted it over Jasper's head and also pushed some of the powder into the headband.

Larson spoke in Cherokee. "Bind us together until the end and make us strong."

Jasper was amazed that he knew what the old man was saying.

"Now, Jasper, you need to remember what I'm saying. And when you feel scared, I want you to say that out loud."

From another drawer Larson pulled a handful of Indian corn and turned to Jasper. He opened the pouch and then poured the Indian corn into the pouch. From another place in the dresser he pulled a feather that had three beads sewn onto it. He also put that in the headband. And last he pulled out a small gourd and put the corn tassel in the gourd.

"Well, that's all that there is to do. When we get there, you do as I do and chant along with me. And when you feel your strength going, repeat 'Bind us together until the end and make us strong.' Do you think that you can do this?"

"Yes, Uncle, I can do this."

Larson and Jasper made their way back to the house.

Larson said, "Well, Jake, I think we are ready to go before it gets dark on us."

"Larson," Jake asked, "just how safe is my grandson?"

"Well, Jake," Larson said, "he should be okay if he can remember what I have taught him and not to get scared. The spirits feed on fear. And he might feel like he can't go on, but I believe that he is strong and he can handle all this just fine."

"Well, Larson, if something should happen, I want you to get him out of there."

"Okay," Larson said. "I will protect him, if he will let me."

So they all set out in the old Jeep and headed up the road to where Jake's cabin was. As they got closer to the cabin, Jasper could feel the spirits and they seemed to be getting stronger. The old Jeep started to sputter and pop, but the old thing held together until they were in the front yard next to the cabin. A fog was forming around the cabin and Jasper found himself saying what Larson had taught him.

Larson instructed Jake and Victor to go back down the road like he had done the previous time he had performed the earlier ritual.

Larson drew a line with his foot across the road and put the powder in the line he had drawn. Jake had given Jasper the necklace that Will Hardy had given him, and when he put it on he felt the power coming from it like Jake had. Jake could hear the voices coming from inside like before. This time Larson had gotten Wilson out of the cabin and Jake was holding him against his chest.

Jake saw Larson and Jasper walk towards the cabin and for a moment he felt like calling out to Jasper to come back, but he let Jasper go on with Larson. Jake said a silent prayer that both he and Jasper would be okay. Jake thought about Alona and what she might say if she knew what was taking place on the mountain.

Jake watched Larson and Jasper make their way to the cabin. He saw Larson stumble and fall and Jasper reach down and help him get up. That scared Jake. He felt like running to where Larson was, but Larson was already standing back up. The voices were getting louder, and Jake could also hear screams coming from within the fog. He could see Larson talking to Jasper, and both of them were taking the gourd and setting fire to the corn tassel inside. Both of them threw something on the porch. Jake noticed that the voices and screams were not as loud as the first time that Larson had done the ritual. He could hear thunder like before, but no rain had fallen yet.

From within the cabin Jake could hear a new sound coming forth, something that Jake had not heard before. The sound was so loud that Jake thought the cabin was going to explode.

Oh, no, Jake thought. *What is happening*?

A smell filled the air, one that Jake knew was the smell of rotten flesh. He could see Larson, who now was on his knees, and Jasper was bent down talking to the old man. Jake saw Jasper stand back up and take the feather from his headband and start to wave it over the gourd. The smoke from the gourd filled up the space where Jasper stood. The voices were starting to get faster and the sound from within the cabin was starting to get even louder and the ground was starting to shake. Jake remembered what Larson had said about the spirits being weak and he wondered if the old man could be wrong.

From inside the chimney, a ball of fire erupted like a bullet and then exploded. A shower of sparks rained down over the cabin.

"Oh, no," Jake said. "I hope that doesn't set fire to the cabin."

Jake looked over at Victor and he could tell by the look on his face that he was scared.

Victor spoke and said, "I'm really scared for Uncle Larson and Jasper, and I believe we should go and help them."

"Well," Jake said, "we can't help them, and I think that they will be okay."

"Okay," Victor said, "but I'm still worried for them."

Then the rain came and Jake could feel the air getting colder. Jake could barely see Larson and Jasper. The old man was lying on the ground talking to Jasper. Jasper knelt down and helped the old man stand up, and both of them turned toward Jake and Victor and they waved.

"Thank God," Jake said. "It seems like both of them are okay."

The wind and rain were slowing down and the fog was starting to lift and the voices were starting to subside. Both Larson and Jasper came over to where Jake and Victor were standing.

"Well," Larson said, "we won the first round. I guess I was weaker than I thought."

The sun had come out and everything seemed to be back to normal.

"We have to prepare for the worst and I need to rest," said the old man.

"Jake," Larson said, "why don't you check the inside of the cabin and make sure that everything is okay."

Jake walked over to the back porch and noticed something on the floor of the back porch. After a moment, he figured out what it was. There were at least 10 kernels of Indian corn and they were burnt to the point that it was hard to tell what they were.

Jasper walked up and said, "That's the corn that we threw there. It's supposed to absorb the fire, and it looks like it worked."

"How are you feeling?" Jake said to Jasper.

"Oh, well, I'm a little tired, but okay otherwise. I'm good. The spirits will be back, and we have to be ready because the spirits will be stronger the next time."

Darkness was coming and Jake hated to see it come. Larson had come out of the old Jeep where he had been resting and spoke to Jake.

"We have to go back to my house and get some more medicine, and we need to hurry."

"Okay, boys, let's go to Larson's house. He needs to pick up more medicine."

The trip to Larson's went well. And after going back into the small building, Larson emerged with a small basket and a war club. He handed the war club to Jasper and pulled a small bag from the basket.

"Jasper," the old man said, "come with me." And both of them went in the house.

"Let me explain about what we have here," he said. "The war club will be used to kill the spirits and send them far away. You will have to hit them at just the right time after they take human form. And they will take human form, and you have to hit them in the head to totally drive them from your papaw's cabin. And if something was to happen to me, you have to do the rest by yourself. In the basket is the strongest medicine I have. The necklace you have on will keep them from harming you. And keep repeating 'Bind us together until the end and make us strong.'"

Larson opened the basket and pulled a small bottle from inside.

"Jasper," Larson said, "this is the blood of my elders, the true medicine that is very strong, and you have to get it on the front and the back door and make a cross with the blood. But first we have to cleanse you and make you a member of the clan that I belong to; we have to become blood brothers."

Larson drew his hunting knife and drew it across his wrist. Jasper saw the knife cut and blood drip off his wrist for a few moments. Larson turned to Jasper and handed him the knife. Jasper tried not to show fear as he took the knife and slowly put it on his wrist. He knew it was going to hurt, so he clenched his teeth and drew the knife across his wrist. The knife was sharp and it cut deeper than he had expected. Larson grabbed Jasper's arm and then put his wrist on his and pressed hard. After a few moments he turned Jasper loose, and then he opened the small jar and let a few drops of Jasper's blood go in the bottle.

"Now, my child, you are part of a society that is many years old," Larson said. "Now we will always be together, and some day we will join your grandmother and her granddaughter. We have to be getting back to the cabin. And one more thing. The spirits will be waiting on you, so you had better let your papaw drive the Jeep back up the road to the cabin. Now, just remember that the spirits can't hurt you, but they will try and make you hurt yourself."

It was already dark out and that made Jasper more scared and scared of what would happen when they got back in the Jeep and headed back down Rocky Creek. Even though Jasper was scared, he felt better and it seemed like he was getting stronger and some of the dread was gone and he felt like everything was going to be okay.

Before they had gotten to the road that led up to the cabin, Jasper could hear the spirits and they sounded like they were crying, "Please go away." Larson turned to Jasper and asked him how he felt and told him again to repeat the chant, "Bind us together until the end and make us strong." Jasper repeated the saying and almost instantly felt better.

As Jake turned up the driveway, he could tell that this was going to be a hard battle coming up. The old Jeep started sputtering and making a sound that Jake had never heard before. It sounded like the old Jeep was screeching and screaming for Jake to stop. Jake never let off the gas because he knew that nothing was wrong with the Jeep and it was the spirits that were screaming.

As Jake neared the cabin, he could see lightning hitting the cabin. It lit the sky up and showed that there were figures all around the back of the cabin. They looked like they were suspended in air with nothing that he could see holding them up.

Jake and Larson got out of the Jeep. Victor and Jasper got out behind them, staying as close to Jake and Larson as they could. From inside the mist and clouds, Jake could hear the voices and the sound of them was like they were everywhere.

Larson turned to Jasper and said, "We better be going. And just remember not to listen to anything that they will say to you. Anything they might say will be a lie."

Jasper followed Larson toward the cabin. The screams were getting louder and the voices were getting stronger. When they arrived at the porch, Larson touched the edge of the house. From within the cabin Jasper heard a voice that he had heard before and it said, "Please don't make us leave from our home."

Larson shouted at Jasper and said, "They are lying to you. Don't believe anything they say."

Jasper was trying to figure out where he had heard the voice, but he couldn't figure out which direction it had come from. Jake also heard the voice and recognized it as being his mom's voice.

Jake went towards Jasper, and when he got next to him he shouted above the noise. "Jasper! Don't listen to that. It's only the spirits trying to fool you into making you think that it's your grandmother's voice."

Larson had moved over to where Jasper was standing, and before long the voice was gone. Jasper looked over at Larson and it looked like the old man was having a hard time standing up. Jasper moved over to where Larson was, and the old man was breathing hard and there was sweat on his brow.

Jasper said, "Do you want to sit down and rest for a bit, Uncle Larson?"

"No, Jasper, we have work to do and I will be okay. We have to get the blood on the cabin."

Larson pulled the small bottle from his satchel and pulled a small rag from his jacket. He was having a hard time breathing as he put a small amount of the blood on the rag.

"Now, Jasper," he said, "you have to take and put the blood on your finger and make an X on the front door of the cabin. I can't go with you, but I will be right here. You need to hurry. I don't know how much longer I can hold up."

Jasper took the small rag that Larson had put the blood on and moved toward the front porch. When he moved toward the steps, the voices started back up and the sound got louder. As Jasper started up the steps, he felt the earth start to tremble. By this time, the windows had started to rattle. When Jasper got to the front door, he could see smoke coming from the doorknob. Larson had gone down to his knees.

"Don't worry," Larson said, "the knob is not too hot. You can put the blood on the doorknob now. And please hurry."

Before Jasper could put the blood on the door, a scream came from inside the cabin. Now Jasper knew who the voice was and that it was his grandma. Jasper almost stopped, but then he heard Larson say, "Remember, it's all in your head and they can't hurt you."

Jasper stuck his finger to the rag that Larson had put the blood on. Then he made a cross in blood on the door. Thunder was making the cabin shake and Jasper knew that he had to get the blood to the back door. He was starting to feel weak and he could see Larson was lying on the ground and didn't seem to be moving. He came down the front porch and started to make his way toward the back porch, when lightning hit a stump next to it. The force of the strike knocked Jasper down to his knees. It took him a few moments to regain his senses and a few minutes to get back to his feet.

Jake had run over to where Jasper was and was holding him as tight as he could.

"Let me go, Papaw. I have to finish this. I have to get the blood on the back door."

Jake released his hold on Jasper.

"Go check on Uncle Larson for me."

Jasper had become a man without even knowing it, and he knew that he had to finish to help Larson out.

Jake went to where Larson was lying and checked on the old man. He could feel a weak heartbeat and his breathing was very shallow.

Jasper took the small bottle from Larson's jacket and placed some more blood on the rag. He slowly started toward the back porch. Then there was another clap of thunder and the lightning hit just above the cabin. The jar from the lightning bolt hit Jasper and it sent him down to his knees again. This time Jasper went on down to his stomach.

Jake again was at his side and held him still on the ground, saying, "No, Jasper. That's enough."

Jasper got back up and ran toward the back of the cabin. He was staggering, but he was getting there. He was feeling so weak that he didn't know if he was going to make it or not. As Jasper made his way around the cabin, another peal of thunder hit above the cabin next to the chicken house. There were feathers flying everywhere and Jasper was trying to make it to the steps. As he made it up the steps, he fell and for a moment thought he was going to pass out. He pulled himself up and took the rag and put his finger in the blood. The lightning had gotten worse and the voices were louder. Jasper found the doorknob and put an X on the doorknob. Then he passed out and fell to the floor.

Jake and Victor had come to the back porch. After a few minutes of putting cold compresses on Jasper, they had Jasper back to sitting up on the back porch. The first thing Jasper asked was where Uncle Larson was. Jake informed Jasper that the old man was sleeping in the Jeep. Jasper finally got up and was looking to see what had happened and found that he could not remember anything; the last thing he could remember was being at Larson's house and he and Larson were doing the ritual of becoming blood brothers.

Jasper did remember the war club and wondered why hadn't he used it, but he couldn't remember seeing what Larson had told him about the spirits taking on human form and he thought to himself, *This is not over with yet. Oh, God, I don't know if I can do this anymore.*

He thought of Larson asleep in the Jeep, and then remembered what Larson had said. "If something happens to me, you will have to finish what we started."

Jasper turned to Jake and said, "We have to get Larson away from the cabin. This isn't over yet."

"What do you mean?" asked Jake.

"Well, it's something that Larson told me back at his house about the spirits taking on human form. Larson gave me a war club, and I forgot it in the Jeep. We need to hurry and get Larson away from the cabin and see what else is going to happen."

He looked at Jasper and said, "Get the war club out of the Jeep and take the bottle and put some blood on the handle. Go back to the cabin and then put the blood on it. Then that will summon the spirits. Be prepared for what they may look and smell like. Don't stop until they are all dead. I mean, they have to be dead to assure that they are all gone and won't come back."

Jake spoke to Larson and said, "How is Jasper doing this, to be only a 14-year-old?"

"Well, Jake," Larson said, "when we were back at the house, Jasper – him and me done a ritual and it let Jasper have powers of the old ways and to be able to see things that we don't. Jasper has seen things that we can't. Jasper has become a man, and he is also a medicine man. He can end this, if he is given the power to do it. It takes some time to get all the powers he will need." Larson said, "I'm all wore out and Jasper will have to go on by hisself."

The old man slowly closed his eyes and fell back to sleep. Jasper walked back to where the cabin was. It seemed like the cabin had gotten smaller, and the air held a sinister presence. Jasper felt a chill go up his back. He took the small bottle and poured some of the blood on the handle, and then he poured some of it on the head of the club. It was like the club had taken a power of its own and Jasper felt the power in the handle of the club. Jasper tried to remember everything that Larson had told him and the saying, "Bind us together 'til the end and make us strong." He repeated the saying over and over in his head until he was sure that he could remember it.

As Jasper made his way back to the front of the cabin, he felt something hit him from the back and he felt like he was falling and he started to fall in the direction of the front porch. Then it was over and Jasper found that he was standing on the front porch with the war club in hand. Then, if by magic, there stood Larson. Jasper could see that the old man was fine and that he held the gourd in his hand and the corn tassel was burning and Larson was saying something about how everything was okay and the spirits were gone. Jasper almost believed what the old man said. Then he remembered what Larson had said about not believing anything that was said, it was a lie.

Jasper drew back the war club and aimed it at Larson's head. Then there was a scream erupting inside the cabin and, at that, the figure of Larson was gone.

From where Jake was standing, he could see Jasper on the front porch. As he had seen the figure vanish, he knew that he needed to do something but couldn't think of anything to do. He moved over to where Victor was standing and saw the worry on Victor's face.

From somewhere in the cabin, Jake heard Jasper screaming, "Please help me, Papaw." Jake immediately started toward the cabin, and then heard Larson's voice, "Come back here, Jake. Don't believe anything you hear. It's all a lie to trick you into going into the cabin. You don't have anything to protect yourself from the spirits and at this time they will kill you."

From somewhere around the cabin there was a crash, and Jake saw Jasper fighting something on the front porch. He could see Jasper swinging the war club, but nothing else was there and Jake knew that the spirits had taken on human form that only Jasper could see. Jake moved over to where Larson lay on the back of the Jeep. The old man looked as if he was going to die any minute.

"Hear me ..." The old man slowly opened his eyes and looked up at Jake.

"Larson, is there anything going to hurt Jasper? I'm worried about him."

"Well, Jake, if he does everything I told him to do, he will be okay. And there is a chance that he might become a spirit, but that's not likely. He is strong and he has the best of my medicine to help him and he has the blood of the elders flowing through his veins. He is a lot stronger than you might believe."

From inside the cabin Jake heard another crash and he looked toward the front porch. With all the lightning, the cabin was easy to see and Jake could see that Jasper was not on the front porch. It was starting to look like the lightning was all in the inside of the cabin. Jake could see Jasper fighting, and it seemed like whatever he was fighting was getting the best of him.

"Larson, are you sure that there is nothing I could do to help Jasper?"

"Well," the old man said, "there maybe is something you could do to help him."

"Okay," Jake said, "what do I have to do?"

The old man sat up in the Jeep and pulled his deerskin bag from his jacket. He pulled a small gourd from the bag. He also pulled a feather with three beads sewn on it. He also pulled out what Jake thought was a tassel from an ear of corn.

"Now listen carefully. Take the gourd and then the feather after you have set fire to the tassel and spread the smoke away from you. After the tassel stops burning, keep sweeping the smoke away from you. But first," Larson said, "I must anoint you with the blood of my elders. Here, Jake, let me see your wrist."

Jake turned his wrist up to where Larson could get to it. Larson took his knife and made a cut on Jake's wrist that made Jake let out a cry.

"Okay, White Man, you got to be strong for your grandson."

From his pouch he took a small bottle, and after taking the top off he let a few drops fall on the cut. He replaced the lid and put it back in his pouch.

"Now," Larson said, "that will make it possible for you to see the spirits that have taken human form and you can help Jasper tell the ones that have turned into human form. Don't pay any attention to what they look like or what they smell like. They are only part human and the dead skin does smell. Now," Larson said, "you need some form of a weapon, and the best thing I can think of is your axe. Now go and help your grandson."

Jake heard another crash from inside the cabin and could see that Jasper was down. Jake knew that he had to get to Jasper as soon as possible. He found his axe and went to the front porch. He took the gourd and set fire to the tassel until the flame was high. From somewhere he heard another scream. Then he heard Larson shout at him and say, "Look out! Behind you!"

Jake turned just in time to see the most hideous creature he had ever seen in his life. The creature was as tall as Jake and the meat on the bones was rotten and falling off. The face was a pile of rotting flesh and in its hands was a war club just like the one that Jasper had. Jake dropped the gourd and swung the ax. When the axe struck the creature's head, it went in to the hilt and blood and rotten meat went everywhere. The creature fell face first onto the porch. Jake hoped that he had killed the creature because he didn't want to hit it again.

Jake stirred the corn tassel and the fire caught back up. He found the feather and started fanning the fire, which was now ablaze, and putting smoke everywhere. He headed towards the front door of the cabin. He could see that the doorknob was smoking and looked to be hot. Then he thought of what Larson had said about something not being what it looked to be. He reached down and touched the door knob and found it was cold to the touch. He opened the door to find that there were two of the creatures occupying the front room.

When one of the two creatures started toward him, Jake raised the axe and came down hard on its head. The creature screamed and fell like a sack of potatoes. The other creature was still coming towards Jake, so Jake kicked the creature in the gut. Then he remembered what Larson had said about hitting them in the head. Jake raised the axe, but the creature was so fast that Jake missed its head and proceeded to cut the creature's arm off just above the elbow. The creature was quick and got back up and came back at Jake. Jake raised the axe again and swung it. The axe came down hard and made contact and went deep in the creature's head. A scream erupted from the creature as it went down and didn't come back up. Jake turned and almost ran into Jasper.

"How many are there in here, Jasper?" Jake shouted.

"I don't know," Jasper said. "I've killed two already, and looks like you have got three more."

The screams were louder and there were more voices than before. Jake was starting to get worried that there were more creatures than they could handle. He hoped that Jasper would be strong enough to keep fighting until they had killed all of them.

Jake was starting to see that early morn had come upon them.

"Wow," Jake said, "time sure does fly by when you're having fun."

Jake's cell phone rang and the caller was, of all people, Alona. *What would possess her to call at this hour?* he thought to himself.

"Hello?" Jake said. "What are you calling at this hour for?"

"Well, Jake," Alona said, "are you all okay up there on the mountain? I was having a bad dream about you and the boys and it woke me up."

"Yes, Alona," Jake replied, "we are all okay. I was thinking about cooking some breakfast with the fresh meat from the hogs."

"Jake," Alona said, "I'm looking forward to some fresh jowls and some brains with eggs."

Jake looked at Jasper and they smiled.

"Jake," Alona said, "what is that noise?"

"Oh, yeah," Jake said, "I had the radio on. It's something that the boys like."

"Well, okay," Alona said. "I'm glad that everything is okay, and I will let you go and cook breakfast."

No sooner than they had hung up, a scream came from upstairs that made Jake and Jasper both jump.

"Wow," Jasper said, "that sounds like one of the groups that I like to listen to."

"Well," Jake said, "I only wish it was the recorded music from your CD. Well, are you up to going up the stairs and seeing what awaits us up there?"

Jake and Jasper were both covered with the blood and rotten flesh.

"Well, I will go first," Jake said.

They both started up the stairs. Another scream split the air, and Jake heard his mom again and she was saying, "please don't make us leave this place. We have nowhere to go. And if you make us go, it will destroy us."

Jake thought again of what Larson had told him about the spirits using any way to trick a person into thinking that it would be someone that they loved.

"Don't believe what they are saying," said Jasper. "It's all a lie to trick you into thinking it's your mom talking to you."

"Well," Jake said, "it sure does sound like my mom."

Jake and Jasper started up the stairs.

Jasper hollered out, "Look out, Papaw, just above you."

Jake looked up just in time to see another creature coming at him. He was too slow to get a good swing at the creature as it hit him hard on the head and he went down on the stairs and everything went black.

Jake could hear the voices again and again, and he heard the voice of his great-great-great-grandmother. She was standing over him.

"Jake, can you hear me?" she asked.

Jake tried to get up, but he was too weak to stand.

"Just lay there," his grandmother said, "and you will be okay in a few minutes."

But Jake protested by saying, "I need to get back to Jasper. He needs my help in killing the spirits in my home."

"Jake, don't even worry about Jasper. He will be okay. He knows that you will be back soon."

"Why am I here again?" Jake asked.

"Well, my son, she said, you needed to come here and rest for a short while. Listen," the old lady said, "the spirits you are fighting are very strong and you need help to destroy them."

"But how can I be here and get help from you?" Jake asked.

"Jake," she said, "you can get help from your elders here at this place if you will let them."

By this time a group of Indians had gathered around where Jake was lying.

"This is your family and they will help you to regain your strength."

"How long have I been here?" Jake asked.

"Well, to others that are waiting for you, it has only been a few seconds. But, really, you have been here for a day."

"Well," Jake said, "then the others are in suspended time ... only two or three seconds have gone by."

An old Indian moved to where Jake laid.

"Jake, this is the medicine man of our tribe and he will help you."

The old man took a leather bag and from it he pulled an eagle feather. When he spoke, Jake could understand his language. Jake spoke and asked, "How is Larson doing? Is he still alive?"

The old man spoke and told him that Larson was still resting and that he will be okay, and when he gets his strength back he will be back to helping Jake with the spirits.

Jake could not believe how tired he was, and before he knew it he was asleep and on the other side.

Jasper was frozen, as if he was able to think but could not move a muscle. The creature was also motionless on the floor. He could not understand why he could not move. *If only Larson was here, he would tell me what I need to do,* he thought to himself.

On the outside of the cabin, Victor was sitting in the Jeep with Larson. It felt like they were both paralyzed.

"Can you hear me?" Victor said to his uncle.

"Yes," Larson said, "I can hear you. We are in suspended time and one of us has gone back in time to an Indian village where the original medicine man is. He is trying to help Jake or Jasper. The reason he is there is to get help from the first true medicine man. I don't know how long he will be there to get help, but whatever happens we will know it soon."

Larson spoke again. "Listen, Victor," he said, "I know this all seems odd to you, but it's the only way that we can take time to rest and everything. The time can only be done by the medicine man. The time's – well, it's all messed up where we are. And when Jake or Jasper are in this time, the reason it is this way is that time can be stopped but only one day at a time." Larson said, "I hope that the medicine man can help Jake or Jasper."

The sun was shining and the screams were quiet for the moment. Victor listened to the old man snoring and said a silent prayer for him to be safe.

Jake opened his eyes and the old medicine man was still sitting by him waving the eagle feather. Jake smelled something and he noticed a small bowl sitting beside him. Jake saw one of the women pick up the bowl and offer it to him.

"You must eat to get your strength back."

Jake then saw who the Indian was. It was his great-great-great-grandmother. And she came over and sat down by Jake. She seemed more beautiful this time, as she smiled down at him. Jake tried to eat the food and it almost came back up. The old man and Jake's grandmother both burst out laughing at him.

"Easy," said the old man. "You are not used to our medicine. But try it slowly and you will be able to take the medicine down."

Jake tried to eat the food that had been given to him, and after a few tries he managed to get it all down. All of a sudden he started to feel better.

The medicine man spoke and said, "That is the best medicine that we have. It has been handed down for many moons and it's the medicine that our elders used many years ago."

Jake said, "How do I repay you for the medicine?"

"No," the old man said, "we give our medicine freely. You, Jake, are our family and one day we will all be together and live here the way the Great Spirit intended us to, where there is no pain and no sickness and no one will take our hunting ground away. That will be a day I will welcome, for my bones are tired and I can't do the things that I used to do. I remember, many moons ago I used to play stick ball, and I had been the champion more times than I can remember."

Jake saw his grandmother coming back with another small bowl. Jake was afraid to ask what it was this time.

"Here," she said as she sat down. "Jake, this may be a little easier on you than it was before."

Jake smelled what was in the bowl and it smelled good. "What is in there?" he inquired.

"Well," the old man said," it's probably better if you don't know what it is."

They all laughed, and Jake tasted the food and it was worse than the one before.

"Eat," the old man said. "It will really help bring back your strength."

Jake was trying not to vomit, but he thought it would be a miracle if he didn't upchuck. Jake's grandmother brought him a container with liquid that looked like water. He tried it, and this was the worst of all. He knew that he needed to take the medicine, even though it tasted like shit and the liquid in the bowl tasted like urine.

Jake picked up the bowl, and with all his might he drank the entire container. Then he picked up the other bowl and washed it down. He grabbed the last bowl and washed down the remains, and then he sat back trying to hold it all down. For a few moments he thought that it was going to come back up no what matter what he did. Then he stood up, and all the Indians that were standing up gave him a pat on the back and started to yell and shout. Jake's grandmother gave him a big hug and smiled at him. Jake was starting to get a sleepy feeling, as everything began to fade.

"Now you must go back to your people. We will be here for you, and if you need us to come to you we will come."

Before Jake could protest, he felt like he was falling, and before he knew it he saw Jasper's face right next to his and felt the stairs under him.

"Papaw," Jasper said, "where have you been?"

"Well, Jasper, I have been to a beautiful place where there is no pain and suffering and we will never grow old. Jasper, it is a beautiful place where we can live in harmony with the earth and everything that lives on the earth and that lives in it."

"Well, I was wondering how Larson was doing. Have you spoken to him?" Jake asked.

"Well, when you were gone, I couldn't see or speak to him. I did hear something that I thought was him and Victor. They sounded like they were talking amongst themselves. And, Papaw, I would love to know what did happen to me and you that made us not be able to move or talk. It felt like we were in suspended animation and we were not getting to fight the spirits like we were."

"Well," Jake said, "I know the part of what we were doing was tough, and I hope this mess will be over and our lives can get back to normal."

"Well, Papaw," Jasper said, "what did you see when you were gone?"

"Well, Jasper, it's hard to explain to you just what did happen. I went back in time – and please don't laugh at what I'm going to tell you."

"No, Papaw. After all I've seen up here today, I will believe anything you tell me."

"Well, okay, Jasper, I will tell you. When I fell on the stairs, it knocked me out. And the first thing I seen was an Indian village. And I met my great-great-great-great-grandmother. I had been there once, when Larson was fighting the spirits right here, and it seemed like I was there for a long time, but it was no time before I came back. My grandmother told me what I needed to do to help and find the bones of my long lost cousin so she can rest in peace. When my grandmother went into the forest to die, her granddaughter followed her and became lost in the mountains and she didn't never find her. So somewhere around here are the bones of my great-great-great-great-grandmother.

"You know, Jasper," Jake said, "I wanted to stay there where everything was so peaceable and there was no fighting and everyone got along good and the hunting grounds were good and there was plenty of food for everyone and plenty of fish to eat."

"Wow, that sounds like somewhere I would like to go."

"Well, Jasper, I look forward to going there when my time here is finished. And I hope you can be there and we can be together.

"Well, I wonder, when is all this mess going to stop. I'm still tired, and I know you are tired. I wonder when they are going to start, or if by some kind of miracle we have gotten rid of them all together."

"Yes, Papaw, maybe it's a trick to make us think that they are all dead.

"Well, Papaw, let's go and see if we can find Victor and Larson and see what they have to say.

"Wow, the creature is still lying on the stairs, but it looks like it is dead."

"Don't get too close," Jake warned. "We don't know what to expect from that hideous creature."

Jake went over to where the creature was lying and put his hand on what was left of its forehead.

"It's cold all right," Jake said. "Well, let's go find Victor and check on Larson."

When they came out of the house and went over to the old Jeep, they found Victor, who was asleep, and Larson was sitting up in the Jeep.

"Well, Jake," Larson said, "did we find out what it was going on? Are the spirits all dead?"

"No, Larson," Jake said, "they are not all dead. They seem to be resting and trying to recoup. We killed three of them, but I'm sure that they will be back to try and kill us like before."

"Or we just leave them alone and let them have this place," Larson added.

"Oh, no," Jake said. "After we have put all the effort into this place, I'm not about to let them take it away from us without a fight."

"Well, that's what I hoped you would say, Jake," the old man said.

"I did find out that my great-great-great-great-grandmother has been watching us all these years. And I met the first medicine man way back in the 1800s. It was so peaceable back there that I didn't want to come back here, but I knew that my grandchildren all loved me and I had to come back here and be with them, not to mention my two sons and Alona." *And Willow Reid*, Jake thought to himself but quickly regretted.

Why did Jake keep thinking about Willow? And then why did he regret it? He couldn't understand why, after having all that he wanted, he still wanted Willow Reid. Sometimes he wished that she didn't even live here. She was a beautiful woman, and so was Alona. *Wow*, he thought, *I've got two women and I can't even handle either one of them. Wow*!

For the likes of himself, he couldn't even tell what he liked about either of them. Most men would give their left nut to have either one of them, but Jake had been the one to screw up a good thing.

Larson was up moving around and he had walked over to the cabin and sat down on the porch. Jasper moved over to where Larson was sitting. When he spoke, Larson knew that there was something other than what was going on around them that was bothering him.

"What's on your mind, young man?" Larson asked.

"Well," Jasper said, "I feel bad about having to kill something, even though it was trying to kill us, and I wish everything had been different."

"I understand what you are saying," Larson said. "I remember how it was to kill someone when I was in Vietnam. You don't ever get used to the feeling."

"What was it like to have to kill someone, Uncle Larson?"

"Well, I remember the first time I was in battle and I seen the enemy and he was coming to where I was in my foxhole. The closer he came, the more scared I became. And at the time he got to where I was, I seen him bring his weapon up, and I done the same thing and fired. When the bullet hit him, half of his head was gone and he fell. Then I had to search him, and I found a picture of a woman and a small child. I never knew who they were, but I always figured that they were his wife and child. Even though it's been a long time since that happened, I still wake up seeing their face."

"Wow," Jasper said, "I bet that is hard to live with that every day of your life."

Jake approached Larson and asked, "What do we do with the bodies of the creatures we killed?"

"Well," Larson said, "if we don't burn the bodies, they will come back."

Larson turned said to Jasper, "Go in the cabin and see if the bodies are still there."

Jasper walked back into the cabin. Then Larson heard him cry out, "They're gone, Uncle Larson. All three of them are gone."

"Okay," shouted Larson. "Watch for them. They will try and sneak up on you."

Then a scream erupted from somewhere in the cabin. Jake heard Larson shout, "Be careful!"

A peal of thunder crashed down next to the cabin and for the first time Jake saw Wilson. He was running towards the cabin and looked like he was trying to get on the back porch. Jake heard himself scream at Wilson to come back. Wilson made his way up the steps and started scratching on the back door. The wind was blowing and Jake took a run at the back porch. He carried his axe and grabbed Wilson as he went into the cabin. The screams were coming faster and the wind was blowing so hard that Jake thought it was going to rip the top off the cabin. The little dog was shaking so bad that Jake thought that he might die of a heart attack. Jake held him close until he started to calm down.

Jake took a survey of the inside of the cabin and saw that there was a coat of moisture all over everything and the place was in disarray. Where Jasper had hit the creature with the war club, he had also hit and busted a lamp at the bottom of the stairs. The wind was screaming, and from somewhere Jake could hear his mom's voice saying, "Please do not kill them." Jake knew that it was not his mom and that she would not do that to him; it was the spirits talking and they were trying to fool Jake into believing that it was his mom.

A shadow flashed and Jake saw a creature come down the stairs, and then the back door came open and Jasper rushed in bearing the war club. The creature that was now coming toward Jasper had a large war club also. Jake took a large swing at the creature and put the axe all the way in its head.

"Look out!" Jasper hollered. "Look out, Papaw, there is another one behind you."

Jake turned and saw not only one creature, but there were two of them there and they were both carrying war clubs.

Jasper came in behind one of the creatures and swung the war club as hard as he could. He heard a crushing sound as he sunk the war club into the creature's skull. Both creatures were now on the floor and they were screaming.

All of a sudden Larson threw open the door and came in with another axe and came down again on the one that was already down.

"Quick," hollered Larson, "we have to get them outside and burn them. Victor is getting some wood and he is going to build us a fire."

"Boy," Jasper shouted, "these things really do stink."

It was a hard task to get the creatures out of the cabin with all the rotten meat falling off their bones. Jake, Victor and Jasper finally got them piled on the fire that Victor had built. The stink was so bad that Victor thought he was going to throw up, but he held on while the bodies burned.

"Keep a lookout," Larson hollered. "They may come from anywhere. Keep a lookout, please, Victor."

For a few minutes nothing happened; it was just the sound of the burning wood and the stink.

"How are you feeling?" Jake asked Larson.

"I'm a little rested, but I feel like I could rest for days."

Jasper asked, "Do you think that might be all of them, Grandpa?"

"I don't know, Son. I hope it is. But still be careful."

"Okay," Jasper said.

"How are you doing, Victor? And do you understand any of this?"

"Well, Papaw, I know that they are mean and they are ugly and they stink."

"One thing," Larson said. "Don't ever tell this to no one – and if you try and tell someone, they will probably laugh at you because they won't understand it – just say it was an Indian thing, and before you know it you will have forgotten all this because, really, it never did happen."

"Papaw," Jasper shouted out, "I see another one on the front porch and there is another one on the back porch."

Jake and Jasper moved toward the front, but before they could get to the front porch the creature had moved back in the house.

"Be ready," Jake told Jasper.

Victor called to Jake and said, "What can I do to help?"

"Well," Jake said, "get the mowing sickle and try and cut their head off."

Victor ran to the corncrib where the mowing sickle was hanging, grabbed it and went toward the creature on the back porch. Larson grabbed a hatchet and was close behind.

"Be careful, son," Larson said. "If we can get them pinned up in the house, we may have a chance."

The creature had also moved off the porch and was going in the house when Larson swung the hatchet with enough force that it knocked out both of its eyes. They fell at an angle, with one looking up and the other one looking down.

"Quickly get outside and get it on the fire before it can come back," Larson said.

Jasper and Jake had followed the creature in the house and pinned it up in the front room.

"Look at it, Papaw. I think it is getting weaker. It keeps stumbling and trying to get away from us."

"Be careful, son." Jake said. "It could be pretending to try and fool us."

At that moment the creature sprang toward Jake. And then Jasper hit it in the back of the head. It sounded like someone busting wood. The creature hit the floor and rolled over with a thump.

"Hurry, Jasper," Jake said, "let's get it out and on the fire as soon as we can."

The creature was spilling part of its brain on the floor and on Jake, and Jasper attempted to move the body to the edge of the porch.

"Be careful," Jasper said as he dragged the creature off the front porch and Victor came over to help. Together they finally got the creature to the fire. And then something happened as the creature was lying there. It started crying and saying, "If you don't stop, we will die," and the tears seemed real at the time. Then, from somewhere, it pulled a large knife and swung it at Victor, but Larson was faster and buried the hatchet deep into its head.

"Get it on the fire," Larson shouted.

With the second creature on the fire and no more in sight, Jasper sat down on the front porch and tried to rest for a few moments.

Larson said, "I think that we have killed all but one, and I'm afraid that this one will be the leader and he will be hard to kill. The other ones were just the helpers, and now comes the badass. It will be mad for us killing its brood and now it is up to it to see that they get repaid for all that we have done to them."

Then, something happened that sounded like the earth was going to split open. The sound was like nothing else Jake had ever heard; it was so loud that he had to put his hands over his ears and it felt like his head was going to explode.

"My God," Jake said, "where did that thing come from?"

Larson spoke up and said, "That is straight out of hell and it's really pissed. We all need to get in here and fight it. It will take all of us to defeat it, and then it may still come back. My jacket," Larson said, "get it for me."

Victor brought the jacket to Larson. Larson reached inside and brought a small bag out.

"This is all I have got. And don't let it get ahold of the bag. One thing I haven't told you is that this bag contains the only medicine that we have. I can't say what will happen, but rest assured it will put up a fight. We need to do a ritual to get ready. Let's hurry before it's too late."

Larson took the bag out of his jacket and started opening it.

"All right, everybody, let's form a circle in the cabin."

They all went into the cabin and stood in front of the fireplace.

"Okay," Larson said, "let's all form a circle."

From the small bag Larson brought out a white powder that looked like sugar. In each one of their hands he put a little of the white powder.

"Now I want all of you to put the white powder in your mouth and all of you hold hands until I say stop."

Jake could hear something in the cabin and he quickly put the powder under his tongue. All of a sudden smoke came out of all of their mouths and Jake heard the creature scream and start to thrash around as if it was in pain.

"Now!" screamed Larson. "Let's find it. This may be the only chance we have to destroy it."

Jake kicked the back room door open and there it stood. It was bigger than the others were and it stood at least seven feet tall. There was blood coming from its mouth and the teeth looked like something out of a rotten hog. It looked like it was trying to keep from falling.

"Kill it!" Larson shouted as he thrust the hatchet into its face, sinking the blade in as far as it would go.

The creature screamed and swung at Larson, hitting him full in the face and knocking him back in the living room. Larson didn't move from where he fell.

Jake came from the back with the axe and caught one creature in the back of the head and buried the axe to the hilt. The creature fell forward and hit the floor. Jasper came in from the side and caught the creature just under the chin. It sounded like someone broke a tree down. Victor was trying to hit it again in the head.

"Oh, God," Jake called out, "someone check on Larson. He looks like he is hurt bad."

Jasper and Victor stood over the creature while Jake went to check on Larson.

"He's okay, boys, just got knocked out for a spell. Okay, boys," Jake said, "let's get this thing on the fire."

"How are we going to move it?" Jasper asked. "It must weigh 600 pounds."

"Boys, go get the horse and bring it up here with the harness and we will pull it out of the house."

Jasper and Victor came back with the horse and brought it into the cabin. They hooked a chain around the legs of the creature and started pulling it across the floor. Just as they neared the back door, the creature came back to life. It made a dive for the horse, and as it went down on the horse there was a sound like someone shooting a pistol.

"What just happened?" Jake asked.

Victor said, "I seen what happened. When the thing jumped on the back of the horse, it kicked him in the head and I think the horse killed it."

"Burn it!" Larson shouted.

Jake and the boys turned to see Larson standing in the door of the cabin.

"Well, good, you are okay," said Jake.

"Oh, yeah, I'm okay. It's hard to kill an old buzzard like me. Yes, let's get this beast on the fire."

After some effort they had the creature on the fire, and all of a sudden it started screaming and thrashing about and then stood up. Jasper swung the war club, catching the creature full in the face, and then it went back down and fell back into the fire.

"Hurry," Larson yelled, "hit it again and send it back to hell where it came from."

Jasper drew back and hit the creature again, and then there was no movement from the creature as it lay there burning. The stink off the fire was almost more than Jasper could stand and he moved away from the fire to where Larson was standing.

"Uncle Larson," Jasper said, "do you think that it is dead?"

"Well, Jasper, I know it is dead," Larson said. "It had to be a medicine man that delivered the last blow to the creature."

"What are you saying?" asked Jasper.

"Well, Jasper," Larson said, "you have become a medicine man. And now you must learn the ways of the medicine man, and I am the only one who can teach you. You have the blood of our elders flowing through your veins and now you cannot deny who you are. I will teach you all that I know, for my time here is short and you have to carry on in my place."

As Jake looked around at the mess that he would have to clean up, he thought, *Well, now my grandson is a medicine man and I will have to tell his grandmother, and I dread that task. I know that she will jump on me, like so many times before, with all the stuff about how he could have been killed and how his mom and dad would have hated him forever. But the fact that he had become a medicine man just might make Alona proud*. Jake sure hoped it would.

Jake moved over to where Larson was sitting on the front porch and said, "You know, Larson, there is one more thing that we have left to do."

"Yes, I know, Jake," Larson said. "We have to help my cousin find the bones of her grandmother. Now that Jasper is a medicine man, he can help us find her."

"Well, Larson," Jake asked, "what does this mean, now that he is a medicine man?"

"Well, Jake," Larson said, "it means that he will have to take my place when I'm gone and he will be able to do the things I did. He can even perform marriages and funerals. And I am going to try and teach him the ways of our people, for I shall be going soon to the spirit world that awaits me."

Jasper and Victor came over to where Jake and Larson were sitting.

"Well, Papaw, don't we need to bury what's left of these creatures?"

"Well, son, the fire will take everything that has happened here and destroy it. Boys, can you two take the horse and put him back up in the pasture and feed him?"

"Sure, Papaw," Jasper said. And away they went.

"Well," Jake said to Larson, "I will take you home if you want me to."

"I think that would be a good idea. I am still really tired and my head hurts where I got hit."

The boys had returned and Jake informed them that he was going to take Larson home and asked if they wanted to go along.

"Heck, yeah, I am going, especially after what all that had happened here," Victor said.

So they all set out to Larson's house. When they passed the old Jeep sitting just below Larson's house, Victor perked up and said, "Hey, Uncle Larson, could we take the old Jeep home with us?"

"Sure thing," Larson replied. "Today is as good a time as any to take it."

"Boys," Jake said, "we've been up for 48 hours. Aren't you all tired?"

"Well, Papaw, I'm not tired," Victor replied.

"Okay then," Jake said. "I think that the front tire is flat, but I've got my air compressor in the Jeep."

"Okay," Larson said, "I will go and find the keys and the title."

After about an hour they had the tire pumped up and had brake fluid in the old Jeep and the chain hooked to the bumper and were ready to take it to Jake's cabin. Victor was behind the steering wheel and Jasper was in the passenger seat. About a mile down the road, Jake hit a rock, and all of a sudden something flew out of the back of the old Jeep and scared Victor so that he almost lost control of the Jeep.

"What was that?" Jake called out sharply, thinking about the creatures and all that had happened earlier in the day. As he slammed on the brakes and was trying to get out of the Jeep, Victor slammed into the Jeep and knocked Jake back into the driver's seat.

"Oh, no," Jasper said, "I think the creatures are back."

By that time, Jake had made his way back to where Victor sat.

"Are you two okay?" he asked.

"Yes, we are fine," Victor said. "I don't know what that was."

"Well, boys, get out and let's see if we can find out what flew out of the Jeep."

Both boys got out and Jake started to look and see if he could find an explanation to what had just happened. When Jake raised up the back seat, a chicken hit him and flew off to the hillside. Under where the chicken had been were two piles of eggs. They all burst out laughing and Jake said, "I guess we have about 12 or 14 eggs that we will have to give back to Larson." The chickens were long gone as Jake placed the seat back down and they set out again for the cabin.

Days went by and Jake spent most of his time canning the hog meat and putting in more firewood, collecting the remaining apples and digging the potatoes. He had been so busy that he hadn't thought much about going up Webb Creek in search of the little girl's grandmother's bones.

Jake had gone to Larson's to see how he was doing and found out that Jasper had been visiting. Larson told Jake that he had been teaching him the ways of the medicine man and that he thought Jasper was ready to go with them up Webb Creek.

Larson and Jake both felt like it was time to put their business where it needed to be. Jake told Larson that he would talk to Alona and see if the boys could come up for a weekend in the near future. Deep down Jake dreaded calling her for what she might say, and it meant another trip to her house, and it did no good to try and explain to the boys that he didn't want to be up there with Alona.

Lately Jake had been thinking a lot about Willow Reid and how she really got under his skin. In a way, Jake felt like if she would come up, he would regret her being there. He asked himself was it what about her that made him get all turned on by just the way she carried herself. And by comparison to Alona – there was no comparison. Both women were very beautiful. And Jake was in love with both of them, but he could only have one of them, and it would be crazy to try and have both of them.

"Wow," Jake said out loud, "what have I gotten myself into?"

Jake hadn't told Alona anything about what had gone on that weekend that the boys had stayed at the cabin. She had questioned him about Jasper going up to Larson's all the time.

"Well," Jake told Alona, "Larson is teaching Jasper to become a medicine man and he seems to like being around the old man."

"Well, just as long as he doesn't get hurt. I think that he is too young to be a medicine man," Alona said.

"Well, Alona, did you know that Larson became a medicine man when he was 13 years old and he was taught by an old medicine man from the Blue clan?"

Alona didn't have too much to say about that.

"And also," Jake said, "he was there when your mom died, and he has been through a lot of things in his life. I know that he carried his medicine when he was in the Marines. He told me about a time when he used it on a soldier and saved his life after the Marine doctor had given up on him.

"I know that Larson would never let Jasper get hurt, if he could prevent it. There are a lot of things that Larson could teach him and also ways that he could help his people when things got rough. I know that Larson has taught Jasper a lot about the plants that can be used for medicine and how he can conjure on someone that was being mean and make things happen to them. I'm sure that Larson has told Jasper that you can also be an evil spirit, and I think that he has taught Jasper to always be on the good side with his medicine."

Jake almost told Alona what had taken place on the mountain when they killed all the spirits, but then he changed his mind when he thought of what she might say about how he could have gotten hurt. Jake wanted to tell her that Jasper had become a man and looked at everything different now and how he had gone from a 14-year-old to a 25-year-old man.

Jake told Alona that he wanted to help Victor work on the old Jeep that Larson had given to Jasper and Victor. Jasper and Victor had always gotten along good, and they would share the old Jeep together.

"Jake, there is something that I want to ask you," Alona said. "Would you come up when the boys and girls are in school?"

Jake felt a chill run up his backbone all the way to the top of his head. Before he could think of what to say, he blurted out, "Okay," and then immediately started to regret it. *Well, I guess I might as well go up there and get it over with,* he thought to himself.

It was about 1:45 p.m. when he arrived at Alona's house. She was on the porch in a beautiful dress that Jake had bought her some years earlier. She came down the sidewalk. When she came up to Jake, she put her arms around him and kissed him. Jake remembered that that was the way she used to kiss him. It felt good, but he wasn't ready to go any further with her. Her cologne brought back memories and it was hard not to sweep her off her feet.

"Whoa," Jake said, "what is going on?"

"Well," Alona said, "I'm just glad to see you."

Immediately Jake knew that she was lying. Usually Alona never said anything like that. Jake saw a hurt look on her face as she backed up.

"I don't know. I was trying to change the way I acted when you came around and I guess I got carried away."

"But it's okay," Jake said. "I enjoyed it, you being that way around me."

"You did?" Alona asked?

Jake could see a sparkle in her eye.

"Yes, I did," Jake admitted.

They both held onto each other and walked up the sidewalk.

"Come on in," Alona said. "I have made some fresh tea, and I have some of the cookies that you used to like."

They made their way into the front room. While Alona was getting the tea and cookies, Jake looked around the front room. It was the same way that it was when he lived there. When Alona came back in the living room, she sat down beside Jake and fixed him some of the cookies and tea. They sat together on the sofa and talked about what they had been doing these past years that they had been separated. Alona put her hand on Jake's and tried to kiss him, but Jake pulled away.

"Why won't you let me kiss you?"

"Well," Jake said, "you know what will happen if we get started. We will end up in the bed. And I can't deny that I want you, but what about afterwards when it's over? How will you feel and how will I feel about the whole experience? I'm just not ready for that to happen. Please understand that I still love you and you are the most beautiful woman that I know. But I'm just not ready to start with something all over again."

Jake could see the disappointment in Alona's face and he felt sorry for her, after calling him all the way out there and nothing happening.

"Alona," Jake said, "please don't be mad at me. I'm just not ready."

Alona smiled and said, "I should have known better than to think I could have you at this time.

"Oh, yeah," Alona said abruptly, "how did Jasper get the cut on his wrist? And I see you have one, also."

Jake took a deep breath and began to tell Alona about what had taken place on the weekend when the boys had spent two days with him and Larson. It took a long time to tell Alona what all had happened. For the most part, Alona had not gotten mad, after telling how Jasper had become a medicine man and how he had become more mature and nothing had hurt him during the time they stayed up there. Alona and

Jake talked for some time, until they heard the school bus stop in front of the house.

"Well, Jake," Alona said, "we might as well tell the boys that I know all about what took place up there."

"Okay," Jake said as both boys and the girls came running in the house. Both girls came running up to Jake and hugged him.

"Wow, Papaw," Kala said, "did you send Jed and Clampett to the promise land?"

"Well, yes, I did – or to say that Victor and Jasper helped send them."

"Okay. You all got chores to do and you all get to it," Alona broke in.

Jake smiled at Alona and said, "You seem to have all of them under control."

When all the kids had left Alona and Jake by themselves, Jake said to Alona, "There is something that I didn't tell you. I guess you have heard the legend of the small child that searches for the bones of her grandmother? I have heard her around the cabin and it's the same sound that I heard when we camped out that time when I was building the cabin."

"Oh, yeah," Alona said, "you told me that you heard a moan up there while I was asleep."

"Yes, that's it. And now I know that me and Jasper and Larson have to go up Webb Creek to where it gets really rough and find her bones. And when we find the bones, then we will have to do a ritual to get her to come there so we can put her soul to rest. And we have to do it pretty quick."

Jake told Alona about how he had passed out and woke up in the village of his past family and his great-great-great-great-grandmother back in the 1800s, and had been shown his cousin and met the elders of his family.

"And then again, when we were fighting the spirits, I went back there to get my strength back," Jake added.

Alona was just sitting there. Then she finally said, "Wow, Jake, that must have been something, to have met all your family way back there."

"Yes," Jake said, "it was really something. And my great grandmother was as beautiful as you are."

"Wow," Alona said. "I guess that it's all right to take the boys with you this weekend and see if you and them can help you find the bones of her grandma."

"Well," Jake asked, "has Victor been saying anything or acting different since they were on the mountain?"

"Well," Alona said, "he seems to be in another world sometimes. But he hasn't said anything about the weekend yet."

"Well," Jake said, "you can tell him that you know all about that weekend and there may be something he needs to talk about."

"Okay, Jake," Alona said, "I will tell him, and let's see if they want to go with you."

Alona got up and went over on the porch, and then Kala came in the room and sat down by her papaw.

"Well, Papaw," she said, "what's been going on up at the cabin?"

"Well, Kala," he said, "I've been putting up things from the garden and putting up firewood. And, as you know, we killed Jed and Clampett and I brought your grandmother some of the meat. You do like pork chops, don't you?"

Yeah," she answered, "we ate some the other day for supper. Papaw, when can me and Sarah come up and spend the weekend like Jasper and Victor get to do?"

"Well," Jake answered, "we will have to see when your grandma will let you go."

"And we want to go and see our Uncle Larson, too," Kala said.

"Well, I think that I can get your grandma to let you go in the near future, if it isn't a weekend to where you have to go and spend with your mom."

"Oh, no," Kala said. "I hate to have to go up there and spend the weekend with her. I always feel so bad when I get back home."

"I'm sorry," Jake said. "One of these days, that will be over with and you can live where you want to."

Sarah had also come into the room and sat down in her papaw's lap and put her arms around him.

"What you been doing up there on the mountain?" she asked.

"Well, as I was telling your sister, I was putting up things from the garden and putting up firewood."

"Well," she said, "if you were to come home, then you would not have to go get firewood so much."

"Well," Jake smiled, "someday I will be here with you all."

"Oh, yeah?" Sarah asked. "I hope it's soon, Papaw. And also," she said, "where are the cats? Are they still there with you?"

"No," Jake answered, "they left a while back and never came back."

"Did something get them?" Her eyes were starting to moisten, and then she really started to cry and wrapped her arms tight around Jake's neck.

"Well, Sarah, I will try and find them when I get back," Jake said.

Alona had come back in with the two boys behind her and saw Sarah holding onto Jake and crying. She came over to where they were sitting and put her arms out and Sarah went to her.

"What's wrong?" Alona asked.

Sarah spoke up and said, "Papaw told me that Curly and Moe had left the cabin and they have not come back, and I'm sad."

Alona took Sarah back to her bedroom and tried to get her to sleep.

"Well, boys, do you two want to go to the cabin this weekend?"

"Oh, yeah," both of them said eagerly, "we would love to go."

Jake turned to Victor and said, "I've told your grandma all about what we went through the last time you went up there. So you can talk to her about anything that you want to. Okay?"

"Sure," Victor said. "And are we going to get to work on the old Jeep?"

"Well," Jake said, "I think that we can start working. And, by the way, we need to take some of my tools from the garage."

Alona had come back into the living room and sat back down next to Jake. She said to Jake, "I don't want you to get those kids' hopes up by telling them you will be back here, if you're not sure if you are coming back. I don't want to get their hopes back up like before."

"I know," Jake said. "I won't do it anymore."

Alona kissed Jake on the cheek and got up and got Jake a bag full of leather britches.

"I know how you love these beans and I hope you enjoy them."

The boys had already gotten their clothes together and were ready to go with Jake. Jake started to kiss Alona but changed his mind after a vision of Willow Reid flashed in front of him.

Oh, shit! Jake thought. *Here we go again*.

They left Alona's house with Victor driving. As Victor drove the Jeep, Jake was thinking about what had gone on while he was with Alona. He thought about the way Alona was dressed and how sexy she looked. He couldn't deny that he wanted to take her to bed. She was his wife and it would have been okay, but something stopped him. What had it been? He wondered if it was Willow Reid. Jake took a deep breath and told himself that he needed to figure out what he needed; both women would not always be there for him.

"Hey, Dad, do you want to stop at Dent's Cafe?" Victor asked.

Jake thought for a moment and finally said, "Sure, son, why not. I could use something to eat. Are you two hungry?"

"Yeah," Jasper said. "It's been a long time since dinner."

They parked in front of Dent's Cafe and went in. The diner was empty except for Bill Lewis, so Jake and the boys got a table next to the front door.

Bill Lewis came over and said, "I'm short on waitresses. They had to fly Willow Reid out this morning at 5:00 a.m. She was hurting in her stomach. I haven't heard anything yet."

Jake felt a knot in his stomach and everything was starting to spin. Finally Jake asked, "Bill, where did they take her?"

"I think that they took her to Judson Memorial. The medics said she was hurting very bad and they thought it could be a kidney stone."

"Okay," Jake said. "Let me give you my phone number. And if you hear anything, please let me know."

"Okay, will do," Bill said.

The boys had ordered cheeseburgers and fries, but Jake had lost his appetite and only got a cup of coffee. Jake cursed under his breath for this happening while he had the boys with him, and he tried to figure a way that he could go to the hospital and see her. He finally decided to go on and see her and let the boys stay in the Jeep.

"Okay, boys," Jake said, "we are going to make a stop at the hospital. A friend of mine got sick early this morning."

Oh, darn it. What a dilemma I'm in, Jake thought.

Judson Hospital sat at the edge of town. After traveling for about 10 minutes, they pulled into the parking lot in front of the hospital.

Jasper turned to Jake and asked, "Who is this friend of yours? Do we know them?"

"I don't think that you know Willow Reid. She works in Dent's Cafe as a waitress."

"Oh, yeah," Jasper said, "I remember her from the last time that we were in there."

"Okay," Jake said. "I will be back as soon as I can. You two can wait in the waiting room if it gets too cold in the Jeep."

Jake found Willow's room on the top floor. When he approached her room, there was a young man standing in front of her room reading from a chart.

"Hello," Jake said.

The young man turned and faced him. It was Jake's doctor and he smiled. Dr. Jarrett was the doctor that had fixed Jake up when he wrecked his patrol car and had to spend nearly two months in the hospital.

"Well, hello," he said. "It's been a while since you were my patient."

"Well, yes, it has been a while," Jake said.

"Are you here to see Mrs. Reid?"

"Well," Jake said, "I was hoping to talk to you about her condition."

"Well," Dr. Jarrett said, "she is a sick lady and we are doing a number of tests on her. I've ruled out kidney stones and I think that there is something bad wrong with her."

Jake felt a wave of nausea sweep over his stomach.

"Well, what can you tell me?" Jake asked.

"Well, you not being next of kin, I can't tell you much."

"Well, can you get ahold of anyone that is close kin to her?" Jake asked nervously.

"Well, we've tried to locate her sister in Charlotte, North Carolina, and we don't have any contact information. Hopefully, when she wakes up we can get it from her. She was in so much pain that we've had to keep her so sedated that she sleeps all the time."

"Well, can I go in and sit with her for a while?"

"Well, sure," said Dr. Jarrett. "She could wake up at any minute."

Jake pushed the door open and walked in. Willow was hooked up to every machine the hospital had. She looked so helpless just lying there with all the crap hooked to her. Jake went over and sat in a chair that was next to the bed and took her hand. She was cold to the touch, so Jake got up and started looking for a quilt to cover her. He found a blanket in the closet and put it over her and then he sat back down.

Her breath was coming in short gasps and Jake was worried that she was going to stop breathing. As he held her hand, all of a sudden she squeezed his hand and then let go and her hand went limp.

Oh, no, Jake thought.

Then she squeezed his hand again. Jake was looking at her face and saw her eyes open, and she smiled at Jake. He squeezed her hand back, and then kissed her slightly on the lips.

"Hey, cowboy, where you been?" Willow asked weakly. "I seem to have gotten sick and they don't know what is wrong. I have been hurting bad. And I think that they have done all sorts of tests and still they can't find nothing wrong."

"I would have been here sooner if I had known," Jake said. "I just found out a few minutes ago from Bill Lewis at the cafe. Can you tell the doctor how to get ahold of your sister in Charlotte?"

"Sure," she said. "Can you get a piece of paper and pen?"

Jake found a small tablet and pen in the nightstand. Willow told Jake her sister's phone number and her address.

"Do you want me to call her?" Jake asked.

"Yes," Willow replied, "I would appreciate it very much. And tell her not to worry. I will be fine when they find out what is wrong."

"Okay," Jake said, "I will go call her right now."

Jake stepped out of the room and went to the lobby to call her. Darlene Reid answered on the second ring. Jake introduced himself and told her that he was calling about her sister Willow.

"Oh," she said, "I have heard of you, and it's all good."

Jake told Darlene what had happened and that the doctors were having a hard time finding out what was wrong with her.

"Oh, no," she said. "I hope it's nothing serious. She was always the strong one in the family. I will get some clothes ready and I will be there first thing in the morning."

"Do you know the way here?" Jake asked.

"No, I don't, but I've got GPS in my car if you will give me the address."

Jake gave Darlene the address and also his phone number. After talking a few more minutes, they hung up. Jake made his way back to Willow's room, and the nurse was in with her when he got there.

"I just came to give Mrs. Reid her medicine."

Jake went to the bed and found Willow asleep. The nurse gave her a shot through her IV.

"What was that for?" Jake inquired.

"It was a pain shot," the nurse said.

Jake sat back down and took Willow's hand. It was still cold to the touch and her hand was limp.

"Oh, yeah," Jake said, "you can tell Dr. Jarrett that I got ahold of her sister in Charlotte and she said that she would be here in the morning."

Jake sat by Willow for 30 minutes and she didn't wake up. He thought about the boys and figured that he should take them on home. He bent over and kissed Willow on the cheek and squeezed her hand. He didn't get a response, so he left her room and headed back down to where the boys were.

Both boys were in the waiting room and were engrossed in a hot rod magazine.

"You boys ready to go?" Jake asked.

"Oh, yeah," they both said at the same time.

"Well," Jasper asked, "how was your friend? Do you know what is wrong with her?"

"Well," Jake said, "they can't find anything wrong with her and she is sleeping a lot. I guess we will have to wait until tomorrow. Then, hopefully, they will know more."

Jake drove the old Jeep up Rocky Branch. When he started up the road towards the cabin, he felt like something was wrong. As he neared the cabin, Jake saw a light in the road and it was shining bright. He stopped just below the light and got out of the Jeep and walked toward the light. A breeze was blowing and the temperature had dropped at least 10 degrees from what it was in town.

From inside the light, Jake could see a form emerging and it was the small child he had seen above Webb Creek. The form approached Jake and came so close that he thought that it was going to touch him. He turned to see Jasper standing behind him. Jasper walked by Jake to where he was caught up in the light. The form seemed to have Jasper suspended in midair.

"Oh, no!" Jake said out loud. "What have you gone and done to Jasper?"

Jasper turned and smiled at Jake. "I'm okay. She just wants you to help her find her grandmother's bones so she can be at peace."

Jasper slowly sank back to the ground and turned and walked back to where Jake was standing.

"Don't worry," he said, "she won't hurt you. We just need to get up Webb Creek as soon as we can."

"Would you?" Jake asked. "You sure have learned a lot from Larson."

"Yes," Jasper said. "And I really enjoyed being around him. He has taught me a lot of things in the past few weeks. You know, I may be able to help your friend who is in the hospital, if the doctors can't find out what is wrong."

Jake felt a chill run up his spine and started to object, but didn't say anything.

"Would you?" Jake said gratefully as he thought himself, "This is some situation we have got here. Willow and Alona aren't exactly friends, and to think of her grandson helping her out wouldn't go over too good. But if Larson was to come and try his medicine on Willow, it might just work and none would be the wiser."

Jake's cell phone rang and it was the hospital. When he answered, it was Dr. Jarrett.

"Hello? Is this Jake?" he asked.

"Yes, it is," Jake said.

"Well, I hate to have to call you at this late hour. It's about Mrs. Reid. She has gotten worse and I don't think that she is going to last much longer."

Jake felt his knees starting to buckle and his breath getting a lot faster, until he thought that he was going to pass out.

"So if you want to see her, you need to come quickly."

"Okay, doc," Jake said. "I am going to bring someone with me, if that's okay."

"Sure," Dr. Jarrett said, "bring them on."

Jake hurried back to the Jeep and yelled to Jasper, "Come on, we are going to go see Larson."

Jake drove as fast as he could on the rough road. Larson was still up when Jake pulled in the yard and turned on the porch light. Before Jake could get to the porch, the door opened and Larson stepped out on the porch.

"Come on in," Larson said. "I was expecting you."

"Wow! How did you know that I was coming?" Jake asked.

"Well, I had a vision this evening and I seen you in the hospital with someone."

"Yes, that's the reason that I came to see you."

"Yes. I am ready to go with you to the hospital," Larson said.

"Okay," Jake said. "We need to hurry and get there."

The road seemed rougher than before and Jake almost ran off of the road.

"Slow down," Larson said. "I feel that she is okay right now, just as long as she doesn't have a bad spell before we get there."

When Jake arrived at the hospital and Larson told Jasper to come with them, Jake started to object but then stopped himself. He just hoped that they could help her.

When they got to the room, Dr. Jarrett was there with his nurse. Jake spoke with the doctor and told him about Larson and Jasper. At first the doctor objected and wanted Willow's sister to give them the okay for Larson and Jasper to be there and to use their medicine, so Jake found Darlene's phone number. She answered on the first ring. Jake explained that Willow was getting worse and that she might not last the night. He explained about Larson and Jasper and that the doctor wanted her okay before they could start.

"Do you think that they could help her?" Darlene asked.

"Well," Jake said, "I know it wouldn't hurt."

"Well, okay. Give him your phone," Darlene said.

Dr. Jarrett took the phone, and after speaking to Darlene for a few minutes hung up and gave Larson the okay to go ahead with their medicine.

"Okay," Larson said in a commanding tone, "everyone leave the room except for me and Jasper."

Everyone started to leave except for Larson and Jasper. Before they left the room, Jake walked over to the bed and kissed Willow on the cheek and squeezed her hand. Jasper looked at Jake and shook his head as if to say Mamaw would not like that at all. Touching Jasper's shoulder, Jake said, "She is my friend," which seemed to bring a smile to Jasper's face.

Jake had noticed that Willow's hand had gotten warmer. He thought that could be from Larson and Jasper being there – or at least he hoped so. Everybody was gathered in the waiting room.

Victor asked Jake, "What would Mom think of all this?"

"Well, son, it may be hard to explain to you, but she is my friend and I care about her very much. I don't expect you to understand what this is all about."

"Okay," Victor said, "we will let it go for now. And I hope that Uncle Larson and Jasper can help her."

Yeah," Jake said, "I sure hope so, too."

The clock in the waiting room said 12:45 a.m. It had been about an hour and a half since Larson and Jasper had started with their medicine. In Willow's room, both Larson and Jasper were getting tired and it was starting to look like they weren't getting any results. Then Willow opened her eyes and spoke to Jasper.

"How long have I been out?" she asked.

"Well, it's been almost two hours."

"Well, I sure do feel better. You two must know what you are doing."

"Well," Larson said, "just take it easy right now. It will take some time for you to regain your strength."

Larson pulled a small gourd from his bag and took the cork out and told Willow to drink all of it.

"It will not taste good, but it will make you feel a lot better."

Willow drank from the gourd until it was empty and then gasped and said, "What was that?"

Both Larson and Jasper laughed.

Jasper told Larson about the light in the road up to the cabin and how the little girl only wanted Larson and Jake to help her find her grandmother's bones so she could be at peace.

Larson said, "We have to get up there and try and find her and then hunt for her grandmother's bones. I think Willow is going to be okay, and I think that it was a spirit that made her sick. It could be from one of the spirits that we encountered at the cabin, one of the spirits that were trying to get back at Jake for killing their kin. They are strong, and the spirits will try and do as much as they can before they are all dead. But I don't think that this will happen again.

"Well," Larson said, "let's go and tell the doctor that she is getting better."

"Okay," Jasper said.

After talking to Willow, they headed out to the waiting room. Jake stood up when Larson and Jasper entered the room and immediately started to ask questions about Willow and asked if he could go see her.

"Well," Larson said, "I guess it would be okay for you to see her after we talk to her doctor."

"Okay," Jake said. "I will go find him."

After a few minutes the door came open and Jake was following Dr. Jarrett and he had a smile on his face.

"Okay," said Dr. Jarrett, "I want to go and speak to her, and then the rest of you all can go on in to her room."

The doctor left the lobby. Jake tried to sit down, but kept getting back up and pacing the floor until the doctor came back and told everyone that they could go on in. Before they left, he told them not to stay too long because she was tired and she needed her rest.

"Okay," they all said at once, and then headed out to her room.

When they all arrived at her door, Jake made sure that he was the first to get in the room. And when he first saw her sitting on her bed, it was all that he could do to keep from breaking down in tears. Willow looked at him and Jake saw the tears forming in her eyes. He lost all control of his feelings and felt like he was going to break down and cry an ocean full. At that moment Jake knew that he was hopelessly in love with her and nothing could change the way he felt about her.

Willow took Jake's hand and squeezed it and said, "You know, Jake Rose, I love you, and I have loved you for a long time."

"I know, Willow. And I love you, too, and I have for a long time, also."

Jake hugged her tight. At that time the door opened and Victor walked in. When he saw Jake with his arms around Willow, a frown came across his face and he turned and went back out.

"Oh, no," Willow said. "I didn't want to hurt anyone, and it looks like I have."

"Well," Jake said, "I will talk to him and see if I can get him to understand."

Willow pulled away from Jake and laid back down on the bed. Jake started to protest, but then didn't and stood up and said, "I will go and talk to him."

Jake found Victor in the lobby with his head in his hands. Jake sat down beside him, and for a few moments neither one of them said anything. Victor spoke first, and Jake could see that he was upset and on the verge of crying.

"Well, Dad, what have you got to say about all this?"

"Well," Jake replied, "I have known Willow for a long time. And I guess that I fell in love with her sometime ago. I don't know how it happened, but it did. And I would never hurt you and your mom, and I'm sorry that I did hurt you."

"Well," Jasper said sharply, "you sure did hurt me and Mom. And I don't think that I want to see you for a while. I still love you very much; I just don't want to see you. I don't know what Jasper thinks of all this, and I hope he doesn't start hating you."

Dr. Jarrett had come back into the lobby and said, "I don't think I have ever seen anything like this. I was positive that she wasn't going to make it through the night. Whatever Mr. Bearmeat gave her, it really turned things around and gave her her life back. You have an awesome grandson and a friend in Mr. Bearmeat. I only wish that I could perform the things that those two perform."

"Yes," Jake said, "Larson is a good man and he can do a lot of things to help other people, and he only does good for other people."

Jasper had also come back in the lobby and sat down by Victor. They both turned to Jake and glared at him.

"Well," Jasper asked, "what are you going to do? Are you in love with this woman, or what?"

"Well," Jake said, "I have tried to explain to Victor how this all happened, and I don't think that he wants to try and understand. You know I didn't start off to hurt anyone. And I'm sorry that this all happened, but try and understand that sometimes things happen without us wanting it to."

"Well, do you still love Mom?" Victor asked.

"Well, I care for her a lot and I hope that she will be happy out there on Snowridge."

"Well, she loves you, Dad, and I don't want her to be hurt by all this."

"Well," Jake said, "I will talk to her and let her know what is going on."

Larson had come into the lobby and had gone to sleep in one of the chairs. Jake turned to the boys and said, "Well, we need to go on to the cabin and see if we can get some sleep."

"I want to go where my mom is," Victor demanded. "And I'm not very sleepy right now."

"Well, Jasper," Jake asked, "what do you want to do?"

"Well," Jasper said, "I think I will stay with you, Papaw."

Victor got on the phone and called Alona and got her to come to the hospital and take him home. Jake was sure that he would tell Alona all that had happened.

Chapter 18

"Well," Jake said, "I am going back to Willow's room to see if I can talk to her for a few minutes before we go."

"Okay," Jasper said. "I will sit here and sleep in one of the chairs."

Willow was asleep when Jake got back, so he sat down on the edge of the bed and started wondering when it was that he had fallen in love with her. There were a lot of things that Jake didn't know about Willow and he thought back to when he had first met her at Dent's Cafe and how, after all these years of knowing her, he had in some way fallen in love with her.

Willow opened her eyes and smiled up at Jake and said softly. "How long have you been here?"

"Well, long enough to know that my love for you is strong and I will never leave or forsake you."

"Well, Mr. Rose," she said, "I have loved you for a long time and I will never stop loving you no matter what. I just don't want to hurt anyone, and I will back away from you if I have to."

"Well, Willow," Jake said, "I hope that day doesn't ever come. Willow smiled at Jake and closed her eyes. He sat on the bed for some time. The door opened and a spitting image of Willow walked in. It was all that Jake could do to keep himself together. He stood up and extended his hand.

"Hello," she said, "I'm Darlene Reid and you have got to be Jake."

"Well," Jake said, "you are right and I'm glad to meet you."

"Well, Willow never told me that you are very handsome," Darlene said.

Jake felt his face turning red and said, "Well, you are very beautiful, and I'm so glad that you are here."

Darlene walked over to the bed and took Willow's hand and bent down and kissed her on the cheek.

"Wow," Darlene exclaimed, "is she okay? She is cold."

Jake hurried over to where Willow lie in the bed and touched her on the forehead. It was cold to the touch. Jake grabbed the switch that called the nurse. He almost yelled into the speaker as he called for the doctor.

In a few moments the door opened and a nurse came running in. She grabbed a blood pressure cuff and started to take Willow's blood pressure and count her heartbeat. The nurse stopped as the doctor came running in.

"No BP and pulse," she told him.

The doctor put on his stethoscope and listened for a few moments and then stopped. The doctor, who Jake did not know, turned to Darlene and said, "I'm sorry, but Mrs. Reid is dead."

Darlene broke down and started to weep and turned to Jake. He put his arms around her. Jake felt the tears start to flow and they came like a river on a rainy day.

The doctor introduced himself as Dr. Farley and told them that whatever had happened would be found in the autopsy.

Jake walked back over to the bed and bent down and hugged Willow and kissed her on the lips, and then the tears fell like spring rain. The doctor covered Willow with a sheet and told them that he would notify the funeral home and they would come and pick her up.

The door opened and Larson walked in. He walked over to where Jake was standing.

"I'm sorry, Jake," he said. "I didn't think that she would make it. She was in really bad shape. I hope you and her got to talk before she passed away."

"Yes," Jake said, "I got to tell her that I loved her, and she told me the same. I want to thank you for giving us that few minutes. It meant a lot to me."

Jasper had come in and walked up to Jake and hugged him and told him that he loved him and that he was sorry that Willow had passed away. Darlene walked up to Jake and put her arms around him and said, "I know that you loved her and right now you are hurting. Do you want to go somewhere and get a cup of coffee?"

"Sure," Jake said. "We will go to where she worked and I can tell her boss about what has happened. I will try and find out if she had any insurance to help with her funeral expenses."

Chapter 19

The cafe was empty and everyone sat at a middle table. Bill Lewis came over and Jake told him what had happened and Jake saw the tears well up in his eyes.

"Do they know what it was that killed her?" he asked –

"Well, they won't know anything until the autopsy comes back."

Jake introduced Darlene to Bill Lewis and she hugged him. Bill said that Willow had been his favorite waitress and that she had been with him for almost 20 years. He told them not to worry about the funeral bill because he would pay for all of it.

"Well, thanks for doing that," Darlene said. "And I really appreciate all you have done for her."

"Well," Bill said, "to tell you the truth, I loved Willow and have for a long time. She was like a daughter to me and I will really miss her."

"Thank you, Bill," Jake said.

Jasper turned to Jake and said, "I won't tell Mamaw or anyone about what has happened."

"Well, Jasper," Jake said, "I will probably tell her myself and not keep anything hidden."

"Okay," said Jasper. "I'm glad that you are going to tell her. I think it's the right thing to do."

Jake spoke further with Darlene and told her what Larson and Jasper had done when they were trying to help her.

"I'm so glad that they gave me the extra few minutes with Willow, and I wish that you could have gotten to talk to her before she passed."

"Well," Darlene said, "I think that it was meant for you two to have that time alone, and that conversation will stay with you forever."

Jake introduced Darlene to Larson and Jasper.

"Is anyone hungry?" Jake asked. "I can't seem to get an appetite right now."

No one was hungry, so coffee was it. No one spoke for a few minutes. Finally Jasper spoke up and said, "Papaw, why don't you take Darlene up to your cabin and show her how beautiful it is up there?"

"Well, if she wants to see it, I will sure take her up there."

"Maybe in a few days, after the funeral is over with," Darlene said.

"Okay," Jake said. "That will help me get it cleaned up. I think that you will like it up there; that is, if you like log cabins with chickens and a horse."

"Well, did you know that Willow and I grew up on a farm?"

"Well, yes, she had told me that," Jake said.

There was so much of Willow in Darlene that it was hard for Jake to keep from calling her Willow and he had to keep saying "I'm sorry" when he called her Willow. Somewhere deep inside he was falling in love with her.

Dang it! Jake thought. *I have to get ahold of myself before I blurt it out and everyone hears me.*

"Well," Darlene said, "if you could guide me toward the local motel, I will get a room."

Jake kept wondering if Victor had told Alona anything about Willow and how long it would be before Alona called and chewed him out. Jake and Jasper had laid down to rest when the phone rang.

Oh, no, Jake thought as he saw Alona's number on the phone.

"Hello?" Jake said.

And then she spoke. "I was calling to say that I'm sorry for your friend and that she had to die."

"Well, thank you. And, yeah, I hated to see her go."

"Is there anything I can do?" she asked.

"Well, no. But thanks for asking. What did Victor tell you?"

"Well, he said that she was your friend and that he thought you might want to be alone but Jasper stayed with you up there."

"Well," Jake said, "I'm okay with him being here with me. I will be okay. And thanks again for calling me."

"Okay," she said. "And you take care of yourself." She then said goodbye and hung up.

Jake laid back down, but he could never go back to sleep. He checked on Jasper, and he was sleeping soundly.

Jake went out to feed the horse and then the chickens. It was a cool day and it felt good. He had canned the hog meat and put it up in the can house and most everything was getting done for the winter. His thoughts went to the little girl and how she was haunting him to help her find her granny's bones so that she could be at peace. He also thought about the creatures that had come out of the cabin and how hard it was to kill them. He wondered, what if some more came back and would he have to burn his place down. He hoped that they didn't come back. He thought about Larson and wondered if the old man could stand another round with the spirits.

Jake went down to his small garage where they had put Larson's old Jeep and started working on it. Wilson came in and piled up on the front seat of the Jeep. Jake got a pad and pen and started writing things down that he would need to start fixing the Jeep. He looked at Wilson, who was sitting up with the hair on his neck standing up. Jake knew that there was something wrong and a chill went up his back and into the back of his neck.

"Oh, no," Jake said out loud. "I think the spirits are back ... or we never killed all of them."

The light in the garage started flickering and then went out. Jake's first thought was that something had happened to the old generator, so he went out to the small shed that covered the water wheel and the generator. The water wheel was turning and all the belts were on the generator and it seemed to be working fine. He went to the barn and turned on the light. It came on as always, so he went back to the garage and found that the light was on and everything seemed to be okay, but the pad and pen were gone.

Jake looked all over the shop and finally found them on the shelf above his toolbox. He reached up and picked up the pad and written on the first page was: "Please leave this place before you get killed." He dropped the pad on the floor and started getting shaky and felt like he was going to pass out. Wilson started to bark and ran across the front seat and jumped out, which wasn't like Wilson at all. Then the dog ran out of the shop.

Jake was starting to get scared and he knew for a fact that the spirits were back. He moved back out of the shop to where Wilson was standing. The little dog was shaking and when Jake reached down to pet him, his muscles grew taut and he backed away from Jake, which was for sure not like him.

Jake stood outside of the shop for some time until he calmed down. He thought about Larson and debated whether to go see him or not. Then he thought of Jasper and wondered if he had learned enough to take on these spirits.

From somewhere Jake heard a moan and he knew that it was the little girl. It seemed like something was going on, but he didn't know what it was. A scream erupted in the garage and Jake heard another moan coming from inside the garage. He forced himself to go back to the garage and look in. There was disarray everywhere and it looked like there had been a fight. There was also dampness everywhere.

What in the hell is going on around here? he thought to himself.

Then Jake knew the little girl's ghost was fighting the spirits. Jake was amazed at what had happened, and for a second didn't believe that the ghost of the little girl could possibly fight the spirits. Then he saw a mist cover the garage and in the mist stood the small child.

She spoke and said, "Please don't be afraid. I will protect you and your family. Please help me find my grandmother's bones."

She reached out and took Jake's hand and held it for a few moments, and then she was gone. Jake couldn't believe what had happened and stood there for what seemed like 30 minutes.

"Papaw" – the sound came from everywhere and Jake turned to see his grandson standing behind him – "what was that sound I heard?"

"Well, Jasper," Jake said, "I think that it was our protector. The little girl told me that she would keep us safe from the spirits."

"Oh, no!" Jasper exclaimed. "Are the spirits back?"

"Yes," Jake replied, "they are back and I think that what you heard was her fighting the spirits. I saw her and she touched me, and it felt so good to know that she can fight for us. Now we have to go up Webb Creek and see if we can find the bones of her grandmother."

"Okay," Jasper said, "when do we go?"

"Well, we have to go get Larson so he can perform a ritual to summon her to Webb Creek."

"Well," Jasper said, "let's go get Larson."

So they set out to Slay Bacon Mountain. Jake let Jasper drive the Jeep, and after racking the transmission a few times they were on their way to Larson's home. Jasper was doing okay until they hit the road that goes up to Larson's house, so he gave up and let Jake drive the rest of the way.

Larson was sitting on the front porch when they pulled up, and he stood up when Jake and Jasper got out of the Jeep.

"Well," Larson said, "what are you two up to?"

"Well," Jake answered the old man, "we have got to try and get up to Webb Creek."

Jake told the old man about what had happened with the spirits and the little girl and how she had fought the spirits. Larson sat back down on the porch. Jake saw Larson take a deep breath.

"Well, I knew this was going to happen sooner or later, and it needs to be sooner than later," Larson said.

"Well," Jake said to Larson, "do you feel like going with us today?"

"Well," Larson said, "I still feel like I could sleep a week, but we can go today if you want to."

"Well," Jake said, "I would like to get this over with if we could."

"Well, okay," Larson said. "Let me get something together and we can go. Come into the house. There is something that I need to get for Jasper."

Inside the house Larson went into one of the bedrooms and came back with a deerskin bag and handed it to Jasper.

"There are some things in this bag that you will need today when we go up Webb Creek."

Jasper looked inside the bag and saw a small gourd and a smaller bag filled with all kinds of herbs and what looked like beans and corn tassel and a small leather bag full of a white powder. Larson told Jasper to keep this close to him at all times.

Jake sat wondering just how much longer they would have to put up with all this before the spirits would be gone for good. All the spirits had put a lot on Jake and he was getting tired of having to deal with everything. He longed for the time when he had lived on the mountain and Willow was alive. He found it hard to believe that she was gone and wondered now what he was going to do without her. He still loved

Alona, but he didn't think that they could ever be together. And now here was Darlene, and she looked so much like Willow that he thought that for some mysterious reason he was falling in love with her and he didn't even know her.

Wow! Jake thought. *How did all this shit happen*?

"Well," Larson said, "are we all ready?"

Jake thought of how Alona had no idea that there was anything between them and he didn't think that he was going to tell her, at least not now.

Everybody got in the Jeep and headed for Webb Creek.

Larson said, "Hope I can remember how to summon the little girl."

Jake asked, "Do you think that you being so tired is hampering you from getting in contact with her?"

"Well," Larson said, "I think that it has something to do with that, but I think that my age is the main problem. I have never had to summon anyone before."

The trip to Webb Creek was short and Jake found a place to park just off Rocky Branch or Rocky Road, whichever you want to call it. They all got out and proceeded to walk up Webb Creek. The road – or trail – was really steep and Larson had to keep stopping to catch his breath. At one point everybody stopped for a few minutes. Jake told everybody where he had been fishing and had the meeting with the little girl.

Larson spoke up and said, "I believe she was trying to show you where to go to find her granny's bones."

The trail had turned into a small path that was littered with rocks. The going was getting rough and the stops were getting more frequent. There were a lot of waterfalls and the places were very beautiful.

All of a sudden the sun went behind a cloud and it became almost dark and they all had to stop. From somewhere there was a sound that arose that Jake recognized. The sound was the moan of the little girl. The moan sounded like it was trying to tell them something.

Larson listened and then said, "She is with us already and she is trying to help us find the location of the bones."

"Well, what does she need us for?" Jasper asked nervously.

"Well," Larson said, "I believe that she is talking with the mind of a 10-year-old and I will have to try and communicate with her and get her to go away and let us find the bones. Then we will call for her."

"What do we do if she gets mad and won't leave?" Jake asked.

"Well," Larson said, "I believe that I can get her to listen to me."

Larson took a small jar from his bag that was filled with something that looked like dried huckleberry leaves. Larson pulled out a few of the berries and crushed them up in his hand. He then tossed them in the direction that the moan had come from. Then he started talking in the Cherokee language. The sky got darker, and then it was dark and a peal of thunder let loose and the wind started to blow. Larson was still talking and even above the wind he could still be heard. This went on for about five minutes, and then the thunder and wind stopped and slowly the sun came out from under the clouds and the day was like before.

Larson spoke up and said, "It took some doing, but I finally convinced her to let us go on and she would wait for us to contact her."

"Where do you think we should start looking for the bones?" Jake asked.

"Well," Larson said, "we should be close around. And let's look for a cave or some rocks that a person could get under."

So they all went to work hunting. They all searched for some time until Larson said, "We may have to go higher up."

They all started up the small path until they got to where there was a large cluster of big rocks.

"You look here," Larson said, "and I will look over there to where there is another big pile of rocks."

Jasper went on up the trail until he found a cave in the rocks. Some rocks covered the opening, so he started to move some of them away.

Then everyone heard Jasper shout out for them to come up to where he was. When everyone had made their way up to where Jasper was, he showed them the cave and the rocks that he had moved. Larson came over and looked in the cave and then pulled out a small flashlight and pointed it toward the back of the cave.

"Come on, everybody, let's move the rocks so I can get in the cave."

Everybody went to work moving the rocks. When the opening was big enough, Larson started to crawl in the cave.

Jasper spoke up and said, "Uncle Larson, would it be okay if I went in the cave? I'm smaller than you and I think that I can find something easier than you."

"Well," Larson said, "I guess it would be better if you went, anyway. If you find anything, don't bother it, just tell me what it is."

Jasper crawled in the cave and had to wait a few minutes for his eyes to adjust to the darkness. Inside Jasper could stand up. He shined the light all around but didn't see anything. The cave went back in the mountain and he moved slowly forward. Then he saw it. For a moment he thought it was a dead animal, but upon more investigation he saw it was a blanket made from deerskin. Jasper slowly picked up the corner and saw the bones. He sat down and pulled more of the blanket off the bones and felt cold air, and then the inside was ablaze with light. Jasper felt a chill go up his back, and yet he was not scared. For some reason he knew what this was. It was the spirit of the old woman.

Her spirit spoke. "My son, I'm glad that you have found my bones, and now my granddaughter can be at rest."

"Am I your grandson?" Jasper asked.

She said, "Yes, you are. And someday you can join us where we will all be happy and there is no more sickness and no more pain. You have become a medicine man and it is your purpose to go about helping people all your life. Don't ever forget who you are."

"Okay," Jasper said. The light receded and the cave was dark again other than the flashlight. Jasper slowly stood and walked back to the opening of the cave.

"Hey, Uncle Larson, I found them and you can come on in."

So Larson slid through the opening and stood up when he was through.

"Back here, Uncle Larson," said Jasper.

Jasper gave the flashlight to Larson and showed him where the bones were. The old man sat down and examined the bones. Jasper told Larson about seeing her spirit and talking to her and that she said that he was her grandson.

"She also told me that it was my purpose here on earth to help people and that someday we would all be together."

Jasper turned to look in the direction of the front of the cave and found Jake standing behind him.

"Well," Jake said, "I see that you have found the bones. Now how do we get the little girl up here?"

Larson spoke up and said, "That will be up to me. Let's go back outside – but wait. Jasper, come here. I want you to seal this place from human sight. I want you to take the gourd from your deerskin bag, and then I want you to take the corn tassel and put it in the gourd and set it on fire. When it's burning, wave the smoke over the bones and chant the chant I taught you."

So Jasper did as the old man had shown him and then sprinkled some of the herbs over the opening of the cave and slid through the opening. Larson took from his bag a small bottle of clear liquid and set it on the ground along with a feather and also a headband. He put the headband on his head and put the feather in the band.

"We need a small fire. Take the gourd from your bag and fill it with some leaves and put some of the clear liquid in it," Larson directed.

So Jasper did what the old man told him. After a few minutes they had a fire going and Larson started chanting and putting some of the corn tassel on the fire.

"Now we have to wait," said Larson. "And, Jasper, I want you to put some of the medicine that is in your gourd on the fire also."

The sky had turned to a yellow haze and the temperature had fallen. The wind started to blow and Jasper put some more of the liquid from the gourd on the fire. The smoke from the fire turned to a dark red and the fire was roaring loudly. From somewhere, Jasper heard a loud voice, but he could not make out what it was saying.

A fog had settled over the front of the cave. Jake felt like this was the same as what was over the cabin when Larson was trying to get rid of the spirits. Jake saw a figure appear like he had seen that day when he was fishing.

Larson spoke and said, "She is here and I need to show her where the bones are."

The figure stepped out of the fog and walked up to where Jasper stood next to the fire.

"It is you that found my grandmother's bones and I want to thank you for all you have done for me."

She took Jasper's hand and led him to the opening of the cave. She looked at him and said, "Will you show me where they are at?"

Jasper slid through the opening, and when he was through he found the girl was already in the cave. Jasper took her hand and led her to the back of the cave. When the girl saw the place where the bones were lying, she went to her knees and started sobbing. Jasper put his hand on her shoulder and gently rubbed her on the back for a few moments. After a few minutes she stood up and hugged Jasper.

"Now I can finally rest," she said.

"But where are you going?" Jake asked.

"Well," she answered, "I am going to where you have been in your mind and I will see my grandmother and my family. And I will wait on you and we can be together forever."

"I know that Larson will be there and Jake will join us someday. There's one thing I want to ask you," Jasper said. "How can you protect us from the spirits that are at Jake's cabin so he can live there in peace?"

"Well," she said, "I promised Jake that I would protect him and whoever is there at the cabin with him, and I will do that for as long as he is there. And when he dies, I will protect whoever lives in the cabin after that."

"Will I ever see you again?" Jasper asked.

"No, but remember that I will be close by if you ever need me." And then she was gone.

Jasper stood in the cave for a few minutes, then finally slid back through the opening.

Larson stood next to Jasper and said, "Well, it looks to be like you are the medicine man and you will be the one I will send when anyone needs help."

They all headed back down Webb Creek and then hopped in the Jeep and took Larson back to his home. Jake and Jasper then headed back to the cabin. Jake asked Jasper if he wanted to go to Willow's funeral with him.

"I will let you go without me," he answered. "She was your friend and I didn't even know her."

Chapter 20

The day of Willow's funeral was dark and damp. It had been raining for the past few days and everything seemed to be wet. The funeral was held in the funeral home and there weren't many people that came. Jake had donated a place for Willow to be buried and everything seemed to be in order. Jake got a friend of his that was a minister to be there to preach the funeral and everything went along as prepared.

Jake sat with Darlene and had to comfort her a couple of times. He saw a couple of people that gave him a snotty look, but he didn't let it bother him. He was at a funeral of a friend and he let it go at that.

When the funeral was over, Darlene rode with him in the Jeep to the gravesite. Jake stood by her until they lowered the casket in the ground. Darlene broke down in tears and Jake held her until the burial was over with.

Darlene asked Jake to take her to the cabin to see how he lived. He told Darlene a lot about what had been happening on the mountain and how his cabin had been haunted by the little girl and how he and Larson and Jasper had found the bones in the cave. He wondered if Darlene believed everything that he said. He asked her if she believed in ghosts. She answered him by saying that she knew that there were a lot of things that couldn't be explained in this world and there were a lot of people that believed there were ghosts.

When Jake and Darlene reached the cabin, Dexter came off the back porch to meet them with his tail wagging. Jake and Darlene sat in the Jeep and talked for a few minutes. Jake told her a lot about himself and how he used to be a police officer and had wrecked his patrol car into the river that went through Judson and his extended stay in the hospital; how he and Alona had been separated for almost three years and he didn't expect them to get back together in the near future.

Darlene told Jake about her previous marriage that had lasted for 10 years and that one day her husband told her that he didn't love her anymore. She said that it had hit her very hard and that she hadn't dated anyone since they had gone their separate ways, which was eight years ago.

"I guess that I hated every man that walked on the face of the earth," Darlene said remorsefully.

She had quit her job and moved in with a friend of hers, until there had been a misunderstanding and she moved out and found a place of her own. She told Jake that she worked as a director of a rest home until it had been shut down, and now she was not working anywhere.

"Well," Jake said, "let's go into the cabin and I will show you how a hillbilly lives."

She laughed and said, "Okay, sure."

Wilson met them at the back door and started jumping up and down on Jake's leg. Darlene started to laugh, and then Wilson started to jump on her leg and started to bark at her. Jake told her about how he had built the cabin and how he had torn down old buildings and chicken houses and old barns and that some of the lumber he sawed on a friend's sawmill that he borrowed.

"Wow," Darlene said, "a jack of all trades."

"Well," Jake said, "I have tried all my years to learn a little of all trades. Let's go see Brutus and you can see what else I can do."

They walked down the hill to where Brutus sat next to the barn. Jake saw Darlene's mouth drop open when she saw Brutus.

"Oh, my goodness. What is this thing?"

"Well, it used to be a school bus in its earlier years."

Then Jake told her that it had been donated to the church a long time ago, and then the preacher had wrecked it on a curvy road en route to another little town, and that it had been given to him and he had started working on it thereafter.

Jake took Darlene over to the barn and introduced her to Commander, and right off he started to lick her hand. Jake got a sugar lump from a jar and gave it to Darlene to give to him.

"Wow," she said, "I really like your horse."

"Well, maybe we can go riding before you have to go back," Jake said.

"Well, I would love to, but I don't have any clothes to go riding in."

"Well, we can fix that. I'm sure that Willow had some that would fit you. And you do need to go to her place and figure out what to do with her things."

Jake saw the tears well up in Darlene's eyes and he thought that maybe he shouldn't have said that and maybe it was too early for Darlene to be concerned with Willow's things.

"Yes," she said, "you are right. I will have to deal with that sooner or later.

"Tell me," Jake said," how long can you stay here?"

"Well," she said, "I really don't have anything to go back to in Charlotte. I did have a cat, but it died. And my landlord is a really good person and she will take care of my things until I come back."

"Well," Jake said, "I will go with you whenever you want to go to Willow's house and go through her things."

Jake and Darlene walked back to the cabin and went in. Jake showed her around and showed her pictures of his mother and father and how his dad was 55 years old when Jake was born. Jake talked about his childhood and how his mom was an alcoholic and the many times he had come home and found her drunk. Jake didn't say anything about what had happened at the swimming hole, and Darlene didn't ask anything else. Jake showed Darlene his bedroom, and they sat down on the edge of the bed and talked for some time.

Gosh, Jake thought as he marveled about how much Darlene looked like Willow and how much he wanted to hold her. Jake looked in Darlene's eyes and said, "I can't get over how you and Willow look so much alike."

Before Jake realized it, he was kissing her and she was kissing him back.

Darlene broke their embrace and said, "I believe that this is too soon for me and I think you should take me back to my motel room.

"Well," Jake said, "I didn't mean to make you uncomfortable."

"Oh, no, you didn't. It's just too fast for me. We just came from Willow's funeral and I have a lot of things on my mind. I think you are a good man, and maybe later we can continue that kiss."

Jake and Darlene headed back to town and Jake pointed out the graveyard where his mom was buried and told her that his dad was buried in the graveyard where Willow was buried.

"Well," Jake said, "I will look around and see if I can find the key to Willow's house. Her purse should be at Dent's Cafe, and I'm sure that Bill Lewis has put it up. I guess that we could stop by and pick it up, if you want to."

"Sure," Darlene said.

The trip to town went faster than Jake wanted it to. He was already enjoying being with her and it really felt good. Jake and Darlene went in Dent's Cafe and got a window seat.

"Are you hungry?" Jake asked. "I think I could eat something."

"Well, yes, I am," said Darlene.

Jake didn't know the waitress that served them. She said, "Aren't you the one that was a friend of Willow's?"

"Well, yes, I was," Jake said. "And I truly do miss her."

Bill Lewis came over with Willow's purse and gave it to Darlene.

"Well, thank you," she said. "Do you know if she had any pets?"

"Well, Bill said, "I don't think that she had any pets ... or none that she ever spoke of. I hope her house key is in the purse."

Darlene opened the purse and after a bit of looking found a key ring with a number of keys on it. Jake and Darlene got something to eat and after paying their tab went back to the Jeep.

Darlene spoke and said, "Why don't we go to Willow's house right now and see what we will have to do?"

Willow's house was on a back street in Judson, and it was a small brown house with shutters on the windows and with flowers planted around it. Jake checked the mailbox and found some letters that were addressed to Willow and a small box that looked like it might have jewelry in it. Darlene went to the front door and after trying two of the keys found the one that fit the door.

The inside of the house was very appealing, with beautiful curtains all through the house. Jake let Darlene go through the house and went out to check out the garage that was connected to the house. The garage door was locked and Jake could see a car inside. There was a small building at the edge of the yard and Jake checked it out and found that it was locked, also. Darlene called out to Jake, and he walked back to the front door.

"Come on back in," Darlene said. "I've got something to show you."

Jake went in and sat down on the couch. Darlene handed Jake the small box and he opened it. Inside was a Zippo cigarette lighter and engraved on the back was "To Jake, my love. I will always love you. Willow."

Jake sat on the couch and read the inscription over and over as his eyes filled with tears. It was like a dam burst and all the pent-up sadness came pouring out and he cried like a baby. Darlene sat down beside him and put her arm around him.

"I'm so sorry," she said, "that you had to find this. And I know now that she truly loved you."

"Oh, goodness," Jake said, "I have so many regrets that I didn't go to her and be with her before this happened, and now I will never know what it would have been like to really love her."

Darlene sat beside Jake for a few minutes.

After gaining his composure, Jake turned to her and said, "I'm so glad you are here, and I wish you could stay for a long time. I feel that if you were here I could try and get my life back in order. You know you could live here if you wanted to. The house will go to you and everything in it.

"By the way, there is a car in the garage. I wonder if it runs or not. Would it be okay to take the keys and open the garage?"

"Sure," Darlene said as she handed him the keys.

It took a few minutes to find the key to the garage. When he opened the door, he was surprised to see a 1961 Starliner made by Ford Motor Company. It looked like it was in good shape under the layer of dust. When Jake looked at the front bumper, he was surprised again. There was a tag on the bumper that said "Jake." Jake turned and saw Darlene looking at the tag on the bumper, also.

"Well," she said, "I think that Willow really had it bad for you."

"I know," Jake replied. "And I wonder where she got it. Maybe there was someone else with the name Jake."

Jake opened the driver's door and sat down in the seat. The inside was clean and there was no damage that he could see. The glove box revealed three letters, and one of them was open. Inside was the title for the car and it had already been signed over to Jake Rose. Jake felt his heart skip a beat and felt like he was going to pass out. He handed the title to Darlene and showed her where to look.

"Wow," she said, "it looks like the car is yours."

"Well," Jake said, "I remember talking to Willow a long time ago about having a car like this when I was a teenager and that I always wanted to own one like it again."

"Well, Mr. Rose, you seem to have gotten your wish."

Jake popped the hood and saw that the entire engine was chrome and the battery was there. The keys were in the ignition, so Jake turned the switch on and turned the engine over. After a few turns, the engine came to life and it made a rumbling noise that Jake really loved.

"Wow," Jake said, "this is really something. All of this is really hard to believe."

Jake turned off the engine and turned to Darlene and said, "If only I hadn't waited to return her love. But I didn't know that she felt that way about me."

"Well," Darlene said, "I know that she was in love with you. It was the only thing she ever talked about when she would call me. I even knew about the car that she had got for you."

"I wonder where she got the money to get it. I know that she didn't make that kind of money by waiting tables," Jake replied.

"Well, when our father passed away, he left us a large amount of money and she bought the car with part of it," Darlene said.

"Well," Jake said, "that explains a lot. And now I know that she would have been there for me in times of need."

"Well," Darlene said, "when are you going to take the car? I know that you can't take it up to the cabin; the road is too rough. You can leave it here if you would like to."

"Well, yes," Jake said, "I think that is a very good idea. And I can come over and wash it. And maybe you and I can go riding sometime."

"Sure," Darlene said. "I would like to do that."

Jake and Darlene checked out the small building in the corner of the yard and found a riding lawnmower, along with a weed eater and some garden tools.

"Well," Jake said, "you will probably have to go to the tax office and check on getting the house put in your name, that is, if you want to come here and stay awhile."

"Well, Jake, I don't really know what I am going to do," she said. "I will have to think about all these things."

"Well," Jake said, "I would like to be a part of your life, if that is possible."

Jake locked up the house and garage and handed the keys to Darlene. She started to take them, but then gave them back to Jake.

"I want you to come by here once in a while and check on everything for me."

"Sure," Jake replied. "I will try and keep the yard mowed, and I will come by and winterize the house before it gets cold."

Jake and Darlene went back to the hotel and went to her room. Jake could see that Darlene had already started packing. They sat down on the couch and talked for a while. Jake was hoping that Darlene would let him kiss her again. He looked into Darlene's eyes and pulled her face next to his and kissed her again. This time she didn't stop him and he kissed her again. Jake reluctantly stood up and said his goodbyes, and then was gone.

Chapter 21

The trip back to the cabin was lonesome and Jake kept thinking about Darlene and Willow. When he arrived at the cabin, he knew something was wrong. There were dead chickens lying everywhere. When he looked at the barn, he could see that the horse was gone. He checked on Wilson and found him on the floor of the cabin. He seemed to be all worn out as if he had been in a fight. Jake looked around and couldn't find Dexter. He looked in the house and under the cabin, but he was nowhere to be found.

Jake sat on the floor and put his head in his hands and thought, *Looks like the spirits are back*. He remembered what the little girl had said about protecting him. This had happened in the daytime, and whatever it was had torn his home all to pieces and nearly killed his small friend. Jake sat by Wilson for a long time and tried to figure out what he should do.

I could go see Larson, I guess, Jake thought. But he didn't really want to bother the old man ... and what exactly was there to do? Larson had used all of his medicine just a few weeks ago and, to Jake, there was nothing that could be done. His thoughts raced. Was he going to have to burn down his home? He didn't want to have to go back to Snowridge. Why hadn't the little girl fought the spirits? Had she been defeated by them?

A voice arose. "I told you that I would protect you and your family from the spirits, but they are stronger than I thought and I am having a hard time when I try and run them away from your home. Your dog is gone, but he will be back. Just have patience for just a little while. I want you to go to sleep and I will send you back to the village to your people. There is a medicine man there that can help you, and you must do what he tells you."

Jake thought for a moment and then said out loud, "There I go again, back to my people. I might as well do it. Then maybe I can find a way to fight all this."

Jake got up from the floor and went over to his recliner and sat down. He was tired, and before he knew it he was asleep.

Chapter 22

The valley was ablaze with the autumn colors and Jake sat looking at the village. He was propped against on a large oak tree and could see the children playing in the valley beside the village. When they saw him, they all came over to where he was sitting. It was the same group that he had seen before.

The oldest boy came to Jake and said, "Hello."

Jake was surprised that he could understand what the boy was saying.

"Hello," Jake said. Then the rest of the kids came up and sat down beside Jake.

"Where are you from?" asked a small girl.

Jake realized that it was the girl that he would have to deal with later on.

"Well," Jake said, "I am from a long way off and I came to visit and to speak to your medicine man."

The oldest boy spoke up and said, "I will go get him so he can talk to you."

"Okay," Jake said. "But first, what is your name?

"Well, my name is Yona, which stands for the bear."

"Well," Jake said, "my name is Jake."

"Okay," Yona said. "I will go get the medicine man."

Before long Jake saw Yona coming back and with him was a gray-haired old man. The old man approached Jake and stuck out his hand.

"Hello," he said. "My name is Jis-tu, which means rabbit, and we are glad that you are here. I hope I can be of help to you."

Jake told the old man about what Larson and Jasper had done when they fought the spirits and how the spirits had come back and had killed all of his chickens and had run his dog off. He also told the old man that there had been spirits that looked like part man and part beast and how the horse had kicked one of them in the head, and that Jasper had finished it off with a war club.

"Well," said the old man, "it sounds like they should be gone from there. Did Larson put down a barrier to ward off any spirits that might come back?"

"Well," Jake said, "I don't think that he did."

"Well, I'm going to give you a potion to put around your cabin and it should keep them away. You need to do as I say for this to work."

"Okay," Jake said, "I will do as you say."

"I will be back with the potion in a short while," the medicine man said. "Why don't you walk around and meet some of your ancestors?"

The old man left and Jake started to walk around. The first person he met was his great-grandmother. She came up and hugged Jake and kissed him on the cheek.

"How are you, my son?" she asked.

"Well, I'm okay, I guess," Jake said, "except I am having to fight the spirits again and I hope that Jis-tu can help me out."

"Well," she said, "he is a powerful medicine man and you will have to listen to him carefully."

"Well, I will listen to him. That's for sure. I seen your granddaughter earlier and she seemed like she is okay now."

"Well, Jake," she said, "Tu-tehia is better now, since you found my bones and she can be at rest after all these years.

"I am so glad that I, along with Jasper, could be of help to her."

Jake looked around at the village, taking it all in.

"I wish that I could stay here with you and the rest of my people," he said longingly.

"I know," Tu-tehia said. "But I see a new love in your life and you would not want to leave her. I think that she loves you and you would be lonely here without her. You must go back and be with your family and grandkids."

"Yes, I know," Jake said.

Jake saw the old man coming back to where he was standing. When he got to where Jake was, he stopped.

"Well, my son," he said, "I have the potion here for you. Now listen to me. You must do this at night when the moon is full. Let there be no clouds in the sky. Start with the corn beads and put them around the outside of your home, and make sure that they are all facing to the sky. The small holes in them should face the house. Next take this deerskin bag and put the sap from the hemlock tree on four sides of your home, and it needs to be facing the north. And last, be sure that the rosin from the mighty pine tree is applied to all corners of your house. That should keep all the spirits away.

"May we see you before long and may your life be full of happiness and your hunting grounds be plentiful. Now, my son, you must go from this place, never to return until it is your time."

Then they were all gone and Jake felt like he was in a tunnel and running toward a light. Then he woke up and found himself sitting in his recliner. Jake sat there for some time and thought about what had happened. In his hand was the deerskin bag the old man had given to him.

Jake got up and went to where his calendar hung and checked when the next full moon would be. The calendar said it would be clear skies and cold weather and it was a week away.

"Oh, no," Jake said. "I hope I can stay here for that long without going crazy. If the little girl could keep them away for a week, then maybe I could put the potion to work."

He wrote down what the medicine man had said so he would not forget. He also wrote down what all was in the potion.

Jake's cell phone rang, but he didn't recognize the number.

"Hello?" Jake said.

"Hey, Jake," Darlene said.

"Oh, hi," Jake said. "Did you have a good trip home?"

"Well, yes, I did. I listened to a book on tape and the name of it was *Whispers*. It's a lot like you, Jake, and I have thought about you all the way home and I seem to be missing you really bad."

"Well, I have thought about you a lot today. Do you remember me telling you about the spirits that are in my cabin? Well, they came back, and when I came home today I found all my chickens dead and I can't find the old dog."

"Jake, are you sure that it wasn't something else that killed your chickens, like a pack of dogs or somebody that came to your cabin when you were with me and done this? I find it hard to believe that it was spirits that done that."

"Well," Jake replied, "I guess that it could be something else that done it ... and I hope it was something else."

"Well," Darlene said, "you could always go stay in Willow's house until you get to the bottom of this."

Jake told Darlene about the potion and when it had to be done.

"Wow," Darlene said, "you went back in time to your people in the 1800s? That is something for you to do. And when you woke up, you were holding a bag of stuff that will ward off the spirits?"

"Well," Jake said, "I could show you the bag that I came back with if you were here."

"Well," Darlene said, "I hope that whatever you brought back will help you get rid of whatever is in your cabin."

"I know that may be hard for you to believe," Jake said, "but there is a lot of truth about the Cherokee legends, and I have seen it firsthand and know how bad the spirits can be."

"Well, okay," Darlene said. "I was just saying that maybe something is haunting your cabin and that you are absolutely right about the spirits. And I know that there are things out there that we can't explain, and I hope that your bag will do the job. I would like to spend the weekend up there when I get back."

Jake felt a chill run up his back with just the thought of Darlene staying at his cabin overnight.

"Well," Darlene said, "I will let you go and fight your spirits. And I hope you win." Then she was gone.

Jake hung the phone up and his thoughts immediately went to Alona out there on Snowridge, and how he needed to tell her to go on with her life, but it was hard for him to let her go, and how this situation could only lead to trouble.

Chapter 23

The weather was turning cold and Jake dreaded it. For some reason his antidepressant wasn't working as it should. It had been over two weeks since Jake had heard from Darlene, and he wondered if he hadn't scared her off with all the talk about the spirits.

The last full moon had been cloudy and he couldn't use the potion that he had brought back. The next full moon was tonight, and according to the weather report it was supposed to be clear and cold. Jake set about getting ready for the night ahead.

He set out for Larson's house to talk to him about the potion and to see if Larson thought it would work. When he arrived at Larson's house, he didn't see the old man anywhere. After knocking on the door, Jake realized that the old man was gone somewhere. As Jake was getting ready to leave, he heard a car coming up the hill to Larson's house. When the car was in sight, Jake saw that it was Alona's Jeep.

"Durn it," Jake said under his breath, "what the hell is she doing here?"

The Jeep pulled up and stopped in front of the house. Alona got out, and then Larson got out of the passenger side.

"Well, hello," said Alona. "What are you doing here?"

"Well," Jake said, "I came to see Larson about us going deer hunting."

"Well, I took Larson to town to get some groceries," Alona said.

"Okay," said Jake.

"Well, it's good to see you," Alona said. "And how have you been doing up here?"

"Well, I guess that I am okay," Jake replied. "And how have you been doing?"

"I'm good," said Alona. "I've been thinking about talking to you. I've decided to go on with my life, since you don't seem to care anything about me or how I am doing."

Jake felt a chill sweep over him but didn't know what to say to her.

"Well, I ..." Jake stuttered, "I didn't think that this would come up this quick, and there is nothing that I can say to you except give me a little more time. There are a lot of things going on with me at this time."

Jake told Alona about the spirits coming back, and that he had gone to his people and the medicine man gave him a potion to use on the cabin.

"Well," Alona said, "Jake, I'm worried about you up here. And these stories you tell are really outrageous. Do you realize how far-fetched they sound?" Alona asked.

"Well, I know for a fact that they are true. If you don't believe me, come over to my cabin and look at all my dead chickens and the mess that everything is," Jake said angrily.

Damn! Jake thought. *She sounds like Darlene.*

"Look, Jake, I will give you a little more time to get this mess over with or I'm gone for good."

With that, Alona got in her Jeep and left.

Jake breathed a sigh of relief and thought to himself, *Why can she do this to me every time that I talk to her*?

Jake then walked up on Larson's front porch and went in the house.

"Well, hello, Larson," Jake said. "I hope that this is okay, for me to come up here."

"Sure, White Boy," Larson said. "Grab a seat and we can talk."

"Well," Jake said, "the spirits are back and the ghost of the little girl said that she isn't strong enough to keep them away from the cabin."

Jake went on to tell Larson about going back in time and that Jistu, the medicine man, had given him a potion to use around the cabin.

"Well, Jake," Larson said, "back a long time ago the medicine they used was a lot stronger than what I had."

Jake went out and got the deerskin bag out of the Jeep and showed it to Larson. Larson looked through what was in it.

"Well," he said, "that will probably work. I have never heard of a potion put together like this, but, like I said, they had stronger medicine back then."

"Well, do you want to come over tonight when I put the potion on the cabin? I need a compass to see which way north is."

"Well," said the old man, "I have a compass that you could use. And if you want me to come over and help put the potion on your cabin, I will."

"Okay. I would like that," Jake said. "And we can cook up some of the hog meat I have canned."

"Well, I can get ready to go. And I'm going to bring some of my medicine, also," Larson said.

Chapter 24

When Jake and Larson got to the cabin, Larson said, "I think if we could purge the land around your cabin, it would help when you put the potion on tonight."

"Okay," Jake said.

So they went to work raking the yard and picking up all the dead chickens.

"Larson," Jake said, "do you think I'm crazy for doing all this? Do I sound like I'm losing it?"

"Well, Jake," Larson said, "I don't think you are crazy, because I seen what the spirits were like when we killed the ones that looked like they were part man and part beast and I know that they were real. A lot of people will not ever believe that the Indian legends are true, and a lot of them will laugh at us if we try and explain it to them."

They went back to raking the yard until they had a path cut around the cabin. Then they got some dry wood and placed it around the cabin. Larson set the wood on fire until it was burning all the way around the cabin. As the fire was burning, both Jake and Larson could hear cries coming from inside the cabin.

"They know that we are going to try and drive them away when we put the potion on the cabin," Larson said.

After the fire had burned down to coals, the cries had stopped. Jake went about putting water on the fire until it was completely out. They propped the rakes up against the cabin and went inside.

Jake started supper. He and Larson talked during supper, and by the time the meal was over it was 7 o'clock and almost dark, and so far there wasn't a cloud in the sky. But something was wrong and Jake could feel it. The air had a strong smell to it and it seemed like there was a fog settling around the cabin.

"What is happening?" Jake asked Larson.

"Well," Larson replied, "it seems like there is more spirits here than was before, and I think they are ready for battle again."

When the clock said 10 o'clock, Jake got out the deerskin bag. Larson lit a torch that he had made before, and they started with the potion. A cry erupted from the cabin as Jake and Larson started with the corn beads, and then all hell broke loose. Thunder erupted and the wind started blowing and it was hard to stand in the wind. Fire started to fly around the cabin and Jake thought that it was going to set the place on fire. Dust blew through the yard and nearly choked them. The old man started to cough and was having a hard time breathing.

"Get in the cabin," Jake yelled to Larson.

But the old man stood his ground. Lightning was striking all around where Jake and Larson were standing.

Larson yelled at Jake, "It wants to hurt you. It's all an illusion. They are trying to scare us off because they know if we succeed they can't stay here."

A peal of thunder crashed and a strike of lightning hit the old man and he went down. Jake ran to the old man lying on the ground and tried to find some sign of life, and there was none. He knew that he had to go on with the potion and hoped that the old man was just knocked out.

Jake made his way around the cabin and placed the corn beads in a row around the cabin. The wind was cold and Jake's fingers were getting numb. Then he took the sap from the hemlock and put it on the four sides of the cabin, and then took the pinesap and placed it on all corners of the cabin. When he had done all this, the wind stopped blowing and the thunder stopped.

It seems like the fog is lifting, Jake thought. And the smell was gone and everything seemed to be back to the way it was.

Jake hurried to where Larson was lying. When he touched the old man, he sprang up and looked at Jake.

"Did we do it?" Larson asked.

"I think we did," Jake said, "or at least for the time being."

Jake helped Larson up and they walked back into the cabin. Jake made a pot of coffee and they sat talking until 2 o'clock in the morning. Larson laid down on the cot and went to sleep. Jake sat in his recliner for some time and waited for something to happen, but all was quiet. At 3 o'clock he got up and went to bed.

Jake's sleep was good and he woke at 10 o'clock. Larson was up and had made breakfast and a fresh pot of coffee. They ate in silence. After their meal, Jake asked Larson where he could get some more chickens to replace the ones that had been killed.

"Well," Larson said, "I can let you have some of mine until you can get some more."

So they headed out to Larson's house.

Chapter 25

After collecting 20 of Larson's chickens and putting them in a cage that Larson had, Jake headed back to his cabin.

When he got back and turned the chickens out, they went everywhere. He started to clean up around the cabin and spotted one of the corn beads beside the cabin that was burnt to a crisp. As he looked, the more beads he found, all the beads were burnt to a crisp.

Wow! Jake thought. *Isn't that something*?

After looking at the cabin, he found that the sap from the hemlock was also burnt and the sap from the pine tree looked like it had been boiled to the cabin.

"Well, I guess it worked after all."

Jake went to the barn and fed his horse. While the horse was eating, Jake noticed a place on the horse's back. The further Jake looked, it seemed like the horse had been burned from the back to down his leg. Jake touched the burnt place and the horse jumped. He found some salve and started rubbing it on the burn. At first the horse kept moving away from him, but finally Jake managed to cover the wound.

I wonder how that happened, Jake thought.

"Well," Jake said out loud, "it must have happened last night during the lightning. But you were locked in your stall. I guess that it came in the stall with you."

Jake spent a few more minutes with the horse and then went back to the cabin. He was tired and was worried about Dexter. He thought about driving around and seeing if he could find the old dog. Wilson was doing better and came over to Jake and jumped up on his lap and went to sleep. Jake relaxed, and before long he was asleep.

Wilson woke Jake up with his bark as he jumped down and ran to the back door. Jake followed and, lo and behold, there stood Dexter. Jake hugged the old dog and then got him some food, which Dexter eagerly ate the whole bowl full and wanted more.

"Okay, Dexter," Jake said, "you have had enough."

Jake sat down on the front porch and looked out over the valley below. The loneliness was coming back and he knew that his depression was coming back and his antidepressant wasn't working anymore. He knew that he needed to go and see Judy Grasson again. He dreaded to have to go see her.

I guess that my meds aren't doing the job anymore, he thought to himself. He had heard that after a while you have to start on a different kind of antidepressant.

Jake thought about Darlene and started to call her, but quickly changed his mind.

What if she doesn't want to talk to me and I'm wasting my time with her? his thoughts rushed in. *And there is Alona out there on Snowridge waiting on me.*

Jake knew that Alona wasn't going to wait forever. He got so mad at himself for being a weak person when it came to dealing with Alona, and he knew that if he went back it would always be like that.

Chapter 26

From somewhere distant, Jake heard a voice that sounded familiar.

"Daddy! Wake up, Daddy!"

Jake opened his eyes and found himself in a hospital bed. When his eyes finally focused, he was looking at his son James. Jake turned his head and saw Alona standing by his bed. She took ahold of his hand and said, "We have been worried about you. Do you remember anything?"

Jake thought for a moment before speaking and then said, "Where am I at? And why are you all standing around my bed?"

"Oh, honey," Alona said, "you were in a car wreck while you were working and you have been in a coma for about six weeks. The doctor wasn't sure if you would come out of it. We have all been praying for you, and I've been here the entire time by your side."

Oh, no! Jake thought, *all this has been a dream*.

Jake started to tremble and thought that he was going to be sick.

"Where is Larson?" Jake asked.

"Don't you remember?" Alona said. "Larson has been dead for over eight years."

Jake felt the tears coming and he couldn't stop them. He cried like a baby.

"Why are you crying?" Alona asked.

Jake felt like he was going to scream and worried that nobody would ever know what he had been through.

"How about my cabin?" Jake asked.

"Honey, you let Charles West stay up there until they could get their house finished."

"Well, I want to go up there," Jake said.

"Okay," Alona said, "after you get to feeling better."

"How about old man Will Hardy?" Jake asked.

"Oh, goodness," Alona said, "he has been dead over ten years, honey."

Jake felt like telling her to shut up and quit telling him that all his friends were dead.

The door to the hospital room opened and in walked Darryl McClain and Jacob Trull.

"Well," Darryl said, "it's good to see you back with the living. I saved your job for you, if you ever feel up to it."

Oh, no! Jake thought as he realized that there was no Willow and no Darlene and all this was a figment of his imagination.

Jake closed his eyes and tried to go away, away up to his cabin with Dexter and Wilson and his horse and his chickens, but deep down he knew that he could never do that.

THE END

Jesus said:

The only ones that shall enter the Gates of Heaven must be born again and believe on me.

And also do the will of my Father: The ten commands.

Be good and Love God with all your heart and mind and soul.

Love your fellow man as I have loved and I gave my life for you so that you may have eternal life.

Pray for each other.

Pray for each for the coming of Jesus Christ is so close.

Just look around you: what Jesus told us in the Bible is happening everywhere. The signs he said are coming true. Read your Bible and give your heart to Jesus before it is too late. He will come as a thief in the night when we least expect it.

May God have mercy on your soul. Think about it. Eternity is forever.

Zack Rose
10-30-18

CPSIA information can be obtained
at www.ICGtesting.com
Printed in the USA
LVHW051119140323
741586LV00004B/321

9 781645 306924